T0166592

PRAISE FOR HAROLD JOHNSON AND *CLIFFORD*

"*Clifford* is a luminous, genre-bending memoir. Heartache and hardship are no match for the disarming whimsy, the layered storytelling shot through with love. The power of land, the pull of family, the turbulence of poverty are threads woven together with explorations of reality, tackling truth with a trickster slant."
— Eden Robinson, author of *Son of a Trickster*

"*Clifford* is a story only Harold Johnson could tell. By turns soft and harsh, intellectual and emotional, Johnson weaves truth, fiction, science, and science fiction into a tapestry that is rich with meaning and maybes. A natural storyteller, Johnson seeks imagined pasts and futurity with equal parts longing and care. This work allows readers and writers the possibility of new and ancient modes of storytelling."
— Tracey Lindberg, author of *Birdie*

"The story's meditations on loss, family, and fateful actions prove absorbing from the opening page."
— *Toronto Star*

THE BJÖRKAN SAGAS

ALSO BY HAROLD R. JOHNSON

FICTION

Billy Tinker
Back Track
Charlie Muskrat
The Cast Stone
Corvus

NONFICTION

Two Families: Treaties and Government

Firewater: How Alcohol Is Killing My People
(and Yours)

Clifford: A Memoir, A Fiction, A Fantasy,
A Thought Experiment

Peace and Good Order:
The Case for Indigenous Justice in Canada

Cry Wolf: Inquest into the True Nature of a Predator

THE
BJÖRKAN
SAGAS

HAROLD R. JOHNSON

ANANSI

Published in Canada in 2021 and the USA in 2021
by House of Anansi Press Inc.
www.houseofanansi.com

25 24 23 22 21   1 2 3 4 5

Library and Archives Canada Cataloguing in Publication

Title: The Björkan sagas / Harold R. Johnson.
Names: Johnson, Harold, 1957- author.
Identifiers: Canadiana (print) 20210222131 | Canadiana (ebook) 20210222158 |
ISBN 9781487009809 (hardcover) | ISBN 9781487009816 (EPUB)
Subjects: LCGFT: Novels.
Classification: LCC PS8569.O328 B56 2021 | DDC C813/.6—dc23

Book design: Alysia Shewchuk

*House of Anansi Press respectfully acknowledges that the land on which we
operate is the Traditional Territory of many Nations, including the Anishinabeg,
the Wendat, and the Haudenosaunee. It is also the Treaty Lands of the
Mississaugas of the Credit.*

With the participation of the Government of Canada
Avec la participation du gouvernement du Canada

*We acknowledge for their financial support of our publishing program the
Canada Council for the Arts, the Ontario Arts Council, and the Government
of Canada.*

Printed and bound in Canada

*For my children, my grandchildren, and the next
seven generations. For this beautiful planet,
for all my relations, and especially
for my relatives, the trees.*

PROLOGUE

"Have you checked on Joe lately?" Joan asked. "I'm worried about him."

"Not yet," I answered.

"Maybe you should."

I looked out at the open water of the river. *Maybe I should*. I hadn't been over to see Joe since the middle of April when the ice was still solid enough to travel by snowmobile. I had been worried then that the ice would be here until June. Spring had come late. We hadn't seen any sign of a melt. The snow in the bush was thigh deep, and when I augered a hole to pump water from the river, the ice was still three feet thick. But when the warm weather finally hit, it hit hard with temperatures in the twenties. A hot south wind and a few heavy rains meant that by the middle of May most of the ice and snow was gone.

I could jump in the boat and be at his cabin in just five minutes if I wanted, but the day was sunny and I was feeling the need to move; I took the canoe. Maybe Joe wouldn't growl and snarl so much if I paddled up to his place. He didn't have much use for modernity, including outboard motors, chainsaws, and snowmobiles.

It felt good to have a paddle in my hands, first time out this year. The river between our place and Joe's is wide where it starts out from the north end of Montreal Lake and begins its winding journey to Lac La Ronge. The cabin Joan and I built is at the very mouth of the river. Joe's place is downstream about three miles on the opposite shore.

Spring and all the birds were back; the ducks and geese and cormorants were busy. A flock of swans, bright white against the brown of last year's rushes, caused me to pull the paddle out of the water, set it across the gunwales of the canoe, and just float for a few minutes to take in their beauty and grace. They wouldn't stay. They were just stopping for a bit of a rest on their journey north. If I was lucky, I might see them again next fall when they headed south for the winter.

There was still a bit of ice on the bay by Joe's place. I had to paddle around the north end and come in nearer the shore to get to his dock. As I walked up to his cabin set back in the pines, it seemed too quiet.

Joan's worry became my worry. Something wasn't right.

"Hey Joe." I raised my voice as I banged on his door.

No answer.

I looked around his yard. There was nothing to indicate anyone had been about recently. His axe leaned against the splitting block by the woodshed. His garden hadn't been touched since the snow melted. That was strange for Joe. He should have done some yard work by now. His little greenhouse looked deserted.

I banged on the door again.

"Hey Joe," I said even louder.

Still no answer.

I tried the door and found it open. I went in. The front room was chilly. Joe's wood cookstove should have been hot. I should have smelled boiled coffee by now. It was mid-morning. I remembered drinking Joe's coffee the last time I'd visited. It wasn't my favourite. He simply boiled water in a pot, threw in a handful of coffee grounds, let it bubble a couple minutes, and then poured it through a sieve into your cup. The sieve didn't catch all the grounds.

The front room was neat. Everything in its place. There was a small, covered bowl on the table. I knew it was full of sugar cubes. Joe liked to put a cube in his mouth and sip hot coffee around it. The table had a red-checkered vinyl tablecloth on it. The green Sony transistor radio was turned off. I envied him that radio. It was old, probably from the sixties or seventies, but it picked up signals better than anything I could buy today. Can't get one of them anymore — and I've been looking.

"Hey Joe." I wasn't quite yelling, but his hearing wasn't that good anymore.

The door to the back room was about a quarter open. I pushed on it and it creaked as it swung back.

Joe was in his bed.

"You a'right?" I asked.

He opened his eyes.

No, he wasn't alright. That much was obvious. It was ten o'clock and he was still in bed. His house was cold.

"I'm not doing so good," Joe said.

"What you want me to do?"

"Not much you can do. I'm just too fucken old." He grimaced, gave a shudder, and closed his eyes again.

"I think you need a doctor."

He took a deep breath. It rattled when he exhaled.

Shit. I should have brought the boat.

Joe wasn't light. I struggled to get him out of the cabin, after I put on his pants, after I cleaned him up. He'd soiled himself. He'd lain still with his eyes closed as I washed him. I knew it was embarrassing for him, so I never said a word. I washed and wiped him, pulled up his pants, put his suspenders over his shoulders, then half dragged and half carried him down to the canoe, where I then struggled to get his legs under the thwart.

We park our vehicles about halfway between our place and Joe's at the old community dock. But I hadn't brought my truck keys with me. I hadn't brought my phone either. If I had I could've called Joan and asked her to come with the boat. I was going to have to paddle home, get my keys, and then come back.

Oh well. Like Joe sometimes said, it was what it was.

A light wind came out of the south, rippled the bright blue water. Nothing serious. It made paddling a bit harder, but with Joe's weight close to the bow, the canoe was easy to steer even with the headwind.

I was across the river from the community dock when I heard the boat coming. It could only be Joan. Montreal Lake was still mostly ice-covered, so no one was coming from the south and there just wasn't anyone else around with a boat.

Ten minutes later she was helping me put Joe in the back seat of her Toyota Highlander. "I knew something was wrong," she said.

The emergency room of the La Ronge Health Centre provided a wheelchair to move Joe from Joan's vehicle to the examination room. It was noon on a Thursday, and they weren't busy. There was one guy sitting in the waiting room, his legs stretched out, his chin on his chest, and his eyes closed. Homeless was my guess, and

· 5 ·

true to La Ronge form, if he wasn't bothering anyone, no one would tell him to move along.

The receptionist wanted Joe's health card.

"Aw, shit," I said. "I never bothered to look for it. It will be in his cabin somewhere."

"Can you get it and phone me with the number later?"

"Yeah, I'll find it." I'd have to ask Joe where it was. I didn't want to go searching around his place uninvited.

"What's his full name?" she asked.

"I don't know," I explained. "I know his real name isn't Joe or Joseph. Julius maybe or something like that. He's from Sweden. So, whatever the Swedes use instead of Joe."

"What's his last name?"

I knew that. "Tossavainen." I knew because that's our original family name as well, from before my dad immigrated and it got changed to Johnson.

"Middle name?"

"I haven't got a clue."

"Birthdate?"

"I don't know that either. But he's old."

I'm sixty-three and Joe's been old as long as I've known him, and that's all my life.

"Are you a relative?"

"Yeah, he's my uncle," I told her. It was sort of true. I thought of Joe as an uncle. He'd been a friend of my dad's. I think dad even helped him emigrate from Sweden. But I'm not a hundred percent sure about that. I remember him coming over to visit at our place, and him and dad sitting outside talking in Swedish, and after he left, dad telling mom that Joe was hard to understand.

"Is it okay if I put you down as next of kin?"

I thought about that for a moment. I guess it would have to be. I couldn't think of anyone else. "Yeah, go ahead," I said.

It struck me then. Joe didn't have anybody. He lived alone in a cabin on the west shore of Montreal River. The same cabin he'd always lived in. I remembered when I was a kid, there had been a woman there, a big woman, and she'd been loud. When I came home in my thirties, there had been a different woman. She didn't say much. But damned if I could remember the names of either of them. As far as I know, Joe never had any children.

Joan and I built our place about twenty years ago. He's our only neighbour. I stop in and check on Joe once in a while. Can't say we really visit. He's not a conversationalist; Joe's more likely to snarl at you than say good morning. In the winter he'll walk over and give me a list of things he needs from town and money to pay for it — salt, sugar, coffee, batteries, bacon. In the summer he comes by canoe.

Whenever I stop in at his place, I check his woodshed to see how much is in there. If it's low I swing by with a sleighload. I put the wood in his shed and leave. He knows I'm there. He would have heard my machine, but he never comes out. Never says thanks. I don't need him to. He never asked me for the wood. I just know that he cuts his with a Swede saw and pulls it home on a toboggan, and I know how tough that is. If I have moose meat I'll drop some off for him. I never offer him fish anymore. I did once and he told me, "I've got my own fucken net. If I want fish, I'll damn well set and lift it myself."

· · ·

Doctor Irvine came out to the waiting room. "I'm going to keep him for a few days. He's dehydrated. But other than being old, there's nothing wrong with him."

Joan and I visited Joe before we left. He was in a room lying flat on his back staring up at the ceiling. There was an IV connected to his wrist.

"They need your health card, Joe. Is it okay if I go into your place and get it?"

He took a deep breath before he spoke. "I don't have one." He closed his eyes. "Never needed one. Never got sick." He took another deep breath. "And I'm not sick now. I'm just old."

"How old are you, Joe?" Joan asked.

He opened his eyes but didn't turn to look at her. He spoke toward the ceiling. "I was born in nineteen…"

She waited a moment, then asked quietly, "Nineteen what?"

He closed his eyes again. "Nineteen," he answered.

"You were born in nineteen nineteen?" It was both a statement and a question.

Joe's silence was his answer. He was over a hundred years old.

"Hey Joe," I said. "We'll come back and check on you in a couple days. Do you want us to do anything for you?"

He was silent for a long time. I took that for his answer and was getting ready to leave when he turned to look at me. His blue eyes were cloudy, and there was a sadness in them in place of his usual defiance. He swallowed before he spoke. "There's a little grey suitcase under my bed. Would you look after it for me? It has important papers in it."

"No problem."

"And make sure the door to the cabin is shut tight."

"I will."

He returned to staring at the ceiling. There was nothing else to say, so we left.

. . .

The little grey suitcase was where Joe said it would be, under his bed, along with an axe handle he hadn't finished carving and a bag that contained scraps of leather. The little grey suitcase looked like it might have been a woman's makeup case back in the forties or fifties. Made of cardboard, it was smaller than some legal briefcases I have lugged. It was definitely old, but despite a few minor scrapes that showed brown underneath the grey, it was in relatively good shape. It didn't weigh much. I gave it a shake, and yeah, it sounded like there might be papers inside.

I took it home and put it on top of the cabinet. None of my business what was in it. Just giving the old guy some peace of mind. It could stay there until he asked for it back.

I didn't sleep well that night. I woke up after a few hours and lay listening to the frogs outside. They're noisy, but I like the sound. If I can hear frogs, I know the environment is still okay. I worry that someday they'll go silent.

It might have been the frogs that woke me up, but it was thoughts of Joe that kept me awake. I didn't know much about him, even after being his neighbour for twenty years. There aren't a lot of neighbours around here. There used to be a community called Molanosa, but the government moved it across the lake and renamed it Weyakwin. Joe stayed put. He wasn't interested in living in a proper house on a street and making monthly payments to the Saskatchewan Housing Authority, even if the house came with electricity and running water.

Joan and I moved here because Molanosa had once been my home. Solar panels provide our electricity, and we can have cellphones and computers. Running water is overrated. We pump water from the river up to a tank in the loft and run a hose down to a sink in the kitchen.

Joe's setup is even simpler. He goes down to the river with a pail when he needs water. In all the years I've known him, I have never seen him use gasoline. I use gasoline to pump my water, to fuel my chainsaw, my lawn mower, my boat, my snow machine, and the generator when there isn't enough sunlight for the solar panels. We also use it in our vehicles.

The only time I ever saw Joe in a vehicle was today when I put him in the back seat. He doesn't have a chainsaw, or a snowmobile, or a boat with a motor. He has a nice little cedar strip canoe that he takes very good care of, and I've seen him carve his own paddles. When I was a kid, I remember he had a dog team; four large, long-haired tan and black dogs that looked like they were built to pull heavy loads. I remember him coming to the house with them. He'd stop out front, tip his toboggan on its side, and his dogs would lie down.

They didn't get up again until Joe righted the toboggan.

It wasn't memories of Joe that kept me awake. It was all the stuff I didn't know about him.

He was a friend of my dad's.

He came from Sweden after the war.

He and Dad spoke Swedish when they were together, but no one knows what they talked about.

Why did Joe come to Canada? And why had he chosen to live in such an out-of-the-way place, across the river from everyone else? Why hadn't he moved to the hamlet? And why was he so grouchy?

Or was he? Was Joe really grouchy or was that just his reputation? I knew he didn't like gas engines, and if you showed up at his house on a snowmobile, he'd snarl at you but wouldn't say anything about the machine. The snarl and the glare said it all. He didn't talk much. He used words sparingly. But then so had my dad. Dad never said anything unless there was something worth saying. Maybe it was a Swedish thing, or maybe it was a generational thing, or maybe it had something to do with the war and the reason he immigrated in the first place.

What was it like to be old and see the end coming?

A lifetime, more than an average lifetime, of being independent, completely independent, and then having someone clean him up after he soiled himself. What must that have been like for him?

How was he doing tonight in the hospital? He said he didn't have a health card because he had never been sick. If he'd never been sick, he'd never been in the hospital before.

It was getting light before I finally fell back asleep. The last thing I remember was looking up at the cabinet and seeing the silhouette of the little suitcase and wondering what might be in there.

. . .

Over the weekend, Joan and I worked on our garden. It was still too early to plant, too great a risk of frost. I changed the oil in the boat, the lawn mower, the generator, and the water pump. It was spring — time to get everything ready. I thought of Joe as I was working; how these were tasks he never had to perform and whether these machines were really making my life any easier.

Monday morning, I told Joan, "I'm going to check on Joe."

"Yeah, you should," she said.

He didn't have anybody else.

I drove the fifty miles to La Ronge to see an old man I wasn't even sure wanted me to visit. But he doesn't have anybody else, I kept telling myself as I drove the old gravel road.

Joe was in bed looking up at the ceiling when I

arrived. When I said, "Hey Joe, how you doing there?" he didn't answer. He just kept looking up at the ceiling, then took a deep breath as though he was going to say something and let it out with a sigh. His shoulders sagged and he closed his eyes.

And I knew.

I don't know how I knew, I just did. He closed his eyes because if he kept them open, he was going to cry.

"Joe, is it okay if I talk to the doctor?"

He nodded. But the nod was very slight.

Doctor Irvine was on duty. I asked him, "What can you tell me about Joe?"

He looked at Joe's file. "You're listed as next of kin, so I can tell you what we know. As far as we can tell, there is nothing wrong with him. He has no infection, no disease; his organs are all functioning. The only thing wrong with him is his heart is slowing down. That's why he doesn't have much strength left."

"What can you do for him?"

Doctor Irvine looked up from the chart. "Nothing," he said. "I can give him medication to increase his heart rate, but at this stage, it might just stop his heart. He's going to be the first person I've seen die of old age. Most people die of some illness they can't fight off. Joe's healthy. It's like his spring has wound down. And we don't have medicine for that."

Doctor Irvine walked with me back to Joe's room.

Neither of us said anything. I was just standing there, trying to think of something to say, when Joe looked at me and said, "Take me home."

I turned to Doctor Irvine. He said, "I don't know if he'll make it home. I don't know if he'll make it to tomorrow. Honestly, I can't even say he'd live any longer if he stayed in the hospital."

"Are you in any pain, Joe?" I asked.

He slowly shook his head. "No, no pain, just some aches of old age. I been lying around too long here. I need to get up and move."

Doctor Irvine helped me get Joe dressed and out to my truck. We reclined the seat a little, and with the seat belt secure, Joe was able to sit up.

"What are you going to do when you get him home?"

"I don't know. Take him to his cabin. Then I guess I'll just hang with him and wait."

"Do you have the number for the coroner?" He wrote it out for me on a sticky, from memory. "When he goes, you phone the coroner right away. Don't touch him until she gets there."

. . .

I kept the speed down on the way back. The road was rough and I didn't want to bounce Joe, but mostly I didn't want to get there.

"Thank you," Joe said. His voice surprised me. "I'm

glad I'm going to die with my pants on. I don't care that I'm wearing a diaper. At least I have my pants on. Maybe when we get home, you'll help me put on a pair of moccasins, eh?"

"Yeah, sure Joe. No problem."

"The way I heard it, after you leave here you have some walking to do, to get all the way over to the other side."

That was probably the longest sentence I'd ever heard Joe speak.

He kept talking.

"That little grey suitcase. You keep what's in there for yourself. There's not much left. I used to have it pretty much full. But you know how it is. The price of fur going to shit the last while, barely worth anything anymore. You know what? I'm glad I'm going. I don't owe anybody a damn thing."

He had to stop and catch his breath. That many words all in a row had taken his energy.

A while later he started to talk again.

"A hundred and one. Not many make it this far. You know what? I never gave anything to the government of Canada, and I never took anything either."

I thought about that. Joe had been a trapper. He sold his pelts and was paid in cash. Nothing for the government to trace, no income tax, but also no pension.

Some things started to make sense: his modest

list of items from town, his insistence on seeing the receipts, and the sour look on his face when he saw the rising prices of those modest items. He didn't have a health card, and for sure he wouldn't have a social insurance number. He'd never owned a vehicle, so he wouldn't have a driver's licence. I suddenly envied him. He was the self-sufficient ascetic that I aspired to be. Only, he had done it and I just talked about it.

"Do you remember seeing an old wolf around these parts last winter?" he asked.

I was trying to think back when he continued, "You remember, he was kind of reddish, more red than tan at least. He used to hang around the river mouth. I'd see him every once in a while, always alone."

"Yeah, I think I know the one you're talking about." I did remember seeing a lone wolf walk past our cabin on the ice.

"I saw where he ended up." Joe took a moment to breathe. "I came across him just as the snow was beginning to melt. The ravens got to him first, and that's how I found him. They'd cleaned him up pretty good, but I was able to read what happened to him." He stopped talking for a couple minutes. I thought he was done, then he said, "He was off the trail about ten feet, underneath a spruce tree. When I found him, I thought, that's a good way to go, just step off the trail, lie down, and curl up to wait for the end. I couldn't ask for better myself."

"Is that what you want, Joe? You want me to leave you under a spruce tree?"

"If you would, please," he answered.

So that's what I did. There was a big old white spruce just a little way down the shore from the dock in front of his cabin. I had to clear away a couple of branches, but I got him sitting up with his back against the trunk. Then I went to find his moccasins.

I'd just finished putting them on his feet, and I was tying up the wraparounds when Joe seemed to levitate for a moment. I wasn't sure what I was seeing, and I moved back for a better look when he slumped onto his side. I was going to help him sit up again, but then I saw it was over. He slowly pulled up his knees and tucked his chin against his chest. His breath rattled gently, and then he was still.

I didn't phone the coroner right away. I waited a few hours to let Joe have some time under the spruce tree, curled up just as he found that wolf earlier in the spring.

I mostly sat on the steps to his cabin but found myself walking down to stand near the spruce tree to watch him lying there. I wondered about what I had seen in those final moments. Had Joe really floated into the air? Had it been real? The more I thought about it, the less certain I became. I convinced myself that it was just my imagination. It must have been the stress of the moment; how often do you get asked to put someone out to die?

. . .

It was late by the time I got home. I told Joan what had happened while I ate the supper she'd prepared.

"What happened with the body?" she asked.

"Coroner took it."

"What are they going to do with it?"

"I don't know."

"Do you think maybe you should find out?"

I was about to say it was none of my business. But if it wasn't my business, whose was it? Someone had to make arrangements for Joe; he couldn't do it. "I'll call in the morning," I said.

. . .

The suitcase. The little grey suitcase was still on top of the cabinet. I was curious to discover what might be in it, but I also didn't want to open it. Maybe because so much had already happened that day, I didn't want to take in any more. Sitting there, watching Joe curled up under that tree, walking away and coming back to sit at a respectable distance, close enough to keep him company, far enough to give him privacy.

I'd experienced a death that day, and a passage, the end of one journey and the beginning of another. Joe, wearing his moccasins, was travelling somewhere, and there is something in that knowing that makes everything else seem less important.

There was money in the suitcase, a lot of money, neat bundles of twenties and fifties. I didn't touch it. There was an envelope on top. I opened that first. It contained three old black-and-white photographs. The first one I guessed right away. It was of Joe's mother, had to be, the age of it, the way she was dressed, in a style common for the twenties or thirties, a stylish hat on her head. She looked like Joe, or I guess Joe looked like her.

I couldn't get a sense of who the people in the other two photographs were. One showed a man in uniform, smiling. I didn't recognize the uniform. Maybe Swedish military? The other was of a beautiful young woman. She was standing on a bridge, leaning on the railing, her head tilted back, laughing, definitely laughing. It was summertime. She was wearing a white short-sleeved blouse tucked into a plaid skirt that came to just below her knees. On the back was scrawled:

To Juha.
    With love,
        Lillian

I moved the money aside. On the bottom of the suitcase were three notebooks. I opened the first and began to read:

Del 1

Frågan

Jag rör om i skålen. Ser köttbitarna i buljongen — substansen av essensen Jag håller skålen mot himlen, minns essencen. Jag hedrar Jorden — spiller lite av buljongen — delar med mig.

    Jag står högt uppe på isen och ser solnedgången,

        absorberas i ögonblicket då ljuset reflekteras

           först mot östra väggen

               studsar tillbaka mot den västra väggen

               tillbaka mot öster

                  och igen till väster

                     tills hela Björka dalen

                       är upplyst av ljuset från

                         isen

                         Ibland

The way the words were laid out on the page, it obviously had poetic elements. The text completely filled the notebook. The other two books were the same; filled with what I guessed to be sagas written in Swedish.

Joan said, "I wonder where he got all the money from."

"The good years," I answered. It was my best guess. "Joe was a trapper back when the prices were decent. In the eighties, a lynx pelt was worth eight hundred dollars. Fisher pelts were up there for a while too. Even beaver pelts paid well. I think he made a whole bunch of money and just never spent it."

There were eighteen bundles. I counted the money in one of them; it contained twenty fifty-dollar bills. A thousand dollars in each bundle. It was a lot of money. Trapping had paid well for a few decades before the big decline. But trapping hadn't died suddenly; it had tapered off. Some species lost value, like the lynx, but others had increased for a time. The marten was the last pelt worth trapping. At its peak, a marten pelt sold for a hundred and fifty dollars. Today, it's barely worth the effort to set a trap. Beaver pelts sell for ten dollars. It's not worth killing an animal like that for ten dollars, unless you plan to eat it.

Joe had lived a lifestyle that didn't require a lot of money. He grew his own vegetables in his garden patch and his little greenhouse. He set a net when he wanted fish. Up until not long ago, he would have been hunting moose and deer. But even in his later years, he could get meat by setting snares for rabbits and shooting the occasional grouse. All he needed money for was salt, sugar, bacon, coffee, and batteries for his radio. I thought about going back to Joe's to get that little Sony radio. And I thought about Joe's cedar strip canoe. If I left them there, someone would come along and take them. But Joe hadn't told me I could take them. He'd said I could have what was in the suitcase, but he never said anything about his other possessions.

. . .

I waited another day before I phoned the coroner to find out what arrangements had been made for Joe's funeral. Like I suspected, nothing had been done. Joe's body was in a morgue in Prince Albert waiting for someone to come claim it. If no one came to claim it, they would bury him at the government's expense.

Joe wouldn't like that. He'd said he'd never given anything to the government and he'd never taken anything from the government.

When the thought *It's none of your business* entered my mind, I pushed it away. My rules, my philosophy, my Cree culture, all those things that told me to mind my own business — don't interfere in another's journey, don't go where you're not wanted — had to be carefully set aside. This *was* my business. It became my business when I went to check on Joe. It became my business when he asked me to take him home to die. It became my business underneath that spruce tree.

And there was no one else. Joe might have had relatives in Sweden, but it was unlikely that I'd be able to find them. I'd found my own relatives in Sweden. But I had the name of the town where my dad came from, Hamra, and I had names to ask about. I knew very little about Joe. Tossavainen isn't a common name. But even if I did find other Tossavainens, I doubted any would remember a man named Joe who'd left Sweden in the early fifties.

No, if anyone was going to make Joe's funeral arrangements, it had to be me.

It didn't take long. A half-hour on the phone and it was all taken care of.

The funeral home would pick up Joe's body from the morgue, take it to be cremated, and have his ashes at the office when I came in to pay for their services on Friday.

Easy enough.

Now for those notebooks. I phoned my cousin Pia in Los, Sweden. It's always good to catch up with her. Somehow, her presence always makes my connection to this planet feel a little more real. Her strong Swedish accent and her laugh that comes from somewhere deep have a grounding effect on me. The only hard part about phoning Pia is that when I hang up, I feel lonely. I immediately want to go back to Sweden and sit in her kitchen and share stories.

"Will you do it?" I ask.

"For you, Harold, I will do it."

I like the way Pia pronounces my name with a soft *A* like in harm, instead of a hard *a* like in hair.

It took me a few hours to scan Joe's notebooks and email them to her.

Pia was quick. It only took her a bit better than a week before she emailed me back the translations along with a note.

Dear Harold,

I'm not certain about all the words. The poem is written in a dialect of Swedish that I am only somewhat familiar with. In Älvaden they speak an older form of Swedish and some of the words are strange to me. But it's not so difficult. Älvaden is only a hundred kilometres from Los and I have heard it spoken before. But even so, in some places I had to guess.

All the best,
Your cousin,
Pia Enocson

THE BJÖRKAN SAGAS

ONE

THE QUEST

I stirred the bowl, found the meat in the broth, the substance in the essence. I held the bowl to the sky and remembered the essence. I showed it to the earth, spilled a bit of broth, shared.

I stood facing the setting sun upon the high ice, absorbed in that moment when sunlight reflects off the top of the East Wall and
    bounces back to the West Wall and
       again to the east and
         again to the west until
           the valley of the Björkan is
             dazzled with light on ice.

Sometimes when the light flashes, if you listen with your heart you might hear music — sometimes, if you listen.

I drank the broth, the essence first because in the

beginning there was only essence. The first story tells us that the essence was lonely. It became substance to give itself a partner. The substance — the meat and the bone — are the next story. We eat them both and remember to be soft like the meat and strong like the bone. The bone that day was quite hard, a sign of things to come.

I saw a woman watching, standing beneath the branches of a björka tree. She would wait until I was done. No Björkan would interrupt another while they ate. I turned my mind back to the bowl — paid attention to the spoon, to the taste. You never know when you might eat again. Hot broth. I paid attention to my breath, my feet on the earth, my legs, my torso, my heart, my mouth, the broth, the meat and the bone. And when I was done, I held the empty bowl to the sky to show there was nothing left. There is a story that says if, when you turn your bowl to the earth, broth or meat or bone falls out, she will know she has given you too much and will hold back her generosity.

I wiped my bowl and spoon and put them in the pocket that only ever holds a bowl and a spoon.

The woman came forward. She kept her eyes down when she spoke. I looked to where the sun had touched the ice in its setting — a bit to the south of pure west, a few days away from the equinox and the change. Today was still in the season of men. Soon it would be the season of women and it would be I who kept my eyes down.

"You are wanted, Juha," she said.

"By whom?"

"The Winter Chief."

THE WINTER CHIEF

I gathered my coat, shut the door to my abode securely, laid my palm against the wood, and said goodbye. You never know when you will be home again. There are stories of men who never said goodbye to their abode, who never returned, and the home became a lonely place.

I love my abode. It was once a björka tree. We waited until it fell. I was allotted a section of the trunk. Before its wood dried out, I carved my home. As I worked on my abode, I recited the stories of promise. I kept my mind the way I wanted my abode to become, kept my mind kind, uncluttered. I put good thoughts into its making — good thoughts that have reverberated for seven winters and six summers. It is a good abode. It provides me with shelter and I know it loves me back.

The woman waited and we walked together. When she looked up, I recognized her: Pia, my dad-sister two summers younger.

Torches lit the way in the fast-failing light to the Winter Chief's abode. The largest section of the largest björka ever to fall in the fifth valley of the Björkan. The entrance was jammed with men. I saw my mom-brothers — Åke and Torn — among them.

I asked, "What's going on?"

Åke shrugged. He did not know.

"The call went out shortly after the zenith." Torn did not know much more.

While we waited, I looked down the slope to where the women were gathered in a half-circle facing us. Politics, I guessed. The time of transference. The Winter Chief had only a few days remaining in his term. At equinox the women would name their Summer Chief. I hoped the call wasn't mere mischief. Torrey had been a good Winter Chief — he had brought us all safely through the dark. He'd been fair in his settles. The long night can bring out the worst in Björkans; a good Winter Chief shines light on the minds of disputants. But it was still days before the transference and mischief had happened before. No wonder the women looked concerned.

I needn't have worried.

"The story trader has not come," Chief Torrey spoke.

I let his words sink in, with all of their implications. If the story trader had not come, then there must be something wrong in the outer world.

"What of the other valleys?" asked a voice from my left that I did not recognize.

"None of the five valleys of the Björkan have been visited this winter. He has not come." So spoke Chief Torrey.

"What shall we do?" asked the voice from my left — it sounded rehearsed.

Chief Torrey stepped onto the altar, walked around the ledge to the front.

He stood in front of the people
    in front of the men
        with the women behind.

"We shall send an ambassador — a scout — to go out of the five valleys, to find, to report."

The voice to my left asked, "Whom shall we send?"

"We will send Juha and two companions of his choosing," answered Winter Chief Torrey.

The men murmured and shuffled their feet. Those near me stepped away.

I stood in a circle of men — all facing me, all watching, all waiting.

I too waited,
    waited for my heart to slow,
        waited for my mind to slow,

waited for my thoughts to form,
to ingest the implications.
And when I was done,
when I had worked it all
through,
balanced the good of
the people with
the good of my
soul,
I spoke: "Thank you for considering me, Winter Chief Torrey. I am honoured to be chosen for such a worthwhile purpose. But I must — in humility — decline."

Chief Torrey stepped to the very edge of the altar, stood straighter. "Tell the people your reasons, Juha, please." He did not sound pleased.

I gathered my words — spoke them in my head — then spoke them aloud. "You are my father and this looks like favouritism."

Sven stepped into the empty circle. "You are not of my blood, Juha. It was I who put your name forward."

Then Ragnar and Jon and Hildor and Sievert entered the circle. Hildor spoke for them. "Neither are you of my blood and we" — he indicated the other four — "accepted and agreed with Sven, and Chief Torrey accepted our recommendation. Thus, you were chosen. There was no favouritism. If you must know, you were selected because among all the people beneath the björka, you best understand the power and the purpose of story."

Even though I had embarrassed myself — or maybe because I had — my words came out of my mouth without edit. "In that case I am honoured to accept this task." I hoped my quick acceptance would distract from what had happened. All five thinkers had identified themselves: Sven, Hildor, Ragnar, Jon, and Sievert. Their task was to advise the chief — their identities should be kept secret so that none would seek to influence. Maybe it didn't matter so much now that we were only days away from the transference. The people would know the thinkers, but it was unlikely there would be important decisions left to be made.

"Choose your companions," Sven said, instead of my father.

Again I made a decision without thinking first. "I choose Torn as my first companion."

It was Hildor who asked, "And your second companion?"

I took time to think. I had chosen Torn because of his abilities with a Björkan blade — his able and willing ways in a fight.

I needed a second — someone to balance Torn's violence. "I choose Sven," I answered.

Thus
  a storyteller,
    a warrior, and
      a thinker
        began an
          adventure.

THE PASSAGE

Someone coughed outside my door before first light.

My mother — Ingra — held a coat. She held it up by the shoulders to show the tree. Turned and showed the back, the other side of the björka tree — its trunk up the spine, its branches across the shoulders and down the arms. Shaped from different-coloured buttons.

She didn't have to tell me.

I didn't have to count:

Two hundred and five.

When she put it on me, I felt the heaviness of its hem.

"Thank you, Mom." I kissed both her cheeks and her forehead. "But it's a bit much."

"One more button would be too much. Make sure you return before they are used up. And when you travel — travel well."

I promised, "I will."

My fingers found the buttons on my chest. A two-hundred-and-five-button coat — she must have been up all night. The outer coat was woven of the thickest björka silk, its lining of the finest. Thinly shaved and dried björka wood covered the vitals: my heart, my liver, and a high collar to protect my throat. Wood shaved so thin it could only have been made by a woman. And smooth — so smooth — it could not have been made with a knife.

"I will give you a story to take with you, my son."

I stepped back.

"It's okay. You can hear women's stories."

She crossed her feet and sat down on the ground.

I crossed my feet and sat as well. I wasn't sure. I was about to hear a woman's story. But Ingra was my mother and I trusted her.

"You know there was a time when there was only Essence, and Essence was lonely and created Substance out of itself."

Yes, I knew that. Everyone did — it's the first story.

"Then Essence and Substance put their minds together and created all the living things. Every plant, every animal is made of both Essence and Substance, and every plant and every animal is male or female. Among the plants, the björka nation is the greatest. It was made first — to shade and protect the smaller plants so that those smaller nations would flourish. The björka is our friend and provides all we need. But its first task — its duty — is to the smaller plants. Among the animals, we are the tallest. We are like the björka and we too have a duty to the smaller animals — to protect them and care for them. And you know all of that."

I nodded.

"It's the first story — the one we are all told — but there is another story, a woman's story. When Essence and Substance were first making plants and animals out of themselves, they only made one gender. The male. They set them on this planet and cared for them, and when a plant or an animal grew old and faded and died, Essence and Substance replaced it with another.

"Then Essence and Substance
    were happy with themselves and
       held each other and
      danced and
        their dancing and
          swirling set the universe in
         motion, and
           as they danced and held
           each other
             something grew
              between them,
               something not
                planned.

"They stopped and looked at this something — wondered at it, at the beauty of it. They took this new something — this spontaneous something that was born from their joining and their happiness — and used it to create the female.

"So, every plant and every animal is either male or female, and in the core of the male — in the core of men and the core of the björka — is the hardness, the strength that stands them up. But the core of the female is made from that mysterious something that came from the lovemaking — the first sex act between Essence and Substance.

"It is that which sets us apart. It is that which makes us female — our ability to take lovemaking and turn it into babies. The first ingredient of the formula for life is love.

"Take this story with you, my son. It doesn't come just from me. The women gathered last night to make you this coat. In our gathering we joined our mysterious something together and used our joining to look into the future. What we saw worried us. So we give you this story to protect you — to keep you safe. Now journey well, my son, and remember to return before you have eaten the last button from your coat."

. . .

We set out just after first light — travelling south along the river. Torn too had a new coat. A new two-hundred-and-five-button coat. I asked him, "Where did you get that fine coat, brother?"

"Why, Juha, my dad-sister Emma brought it to me this morning before first light." He smiled.

"And did she by chance give you a story with it?"

"No." His smile was instantly gone, replaced with a face that looked insulted. Torn was a warrior. He did not know any women's stories.

The fifth valley of the Björkan narrows at its southern end. There the ice walls are high and sheer.

Ice blue and
   sky blue meet
      a hundred tree lengths above
         the stony ground.
           River blue turns itself white as
            it tumbles over stones.

In the height of summer, as the ice melts, the river runs full. At the end of our valley — at the end of the woods — the river runs between the ice walls, and in midsummer when the river is full, it fills the valley and no one can travel in or out through the chasm.

In midsummer, when women hold the balance — when the forest is in bloom and life is flourishing — the river fills the entrance to our valley. It seals us in and seals our enemies out.

By mid-morning we were deep in the chasm. We walked the narrow edge between water and ice, in the depths where the sun leaves the river to tumult in shadow.

By midday we had reached the confluence. There the five rivers of the five valleys come together and there are five garrisons manned by warriors from each of the five valleys.

We stopped. Officially to state our purpose. Unofficially so Torn could visit with his buddies — to tease and joke and tell a few fine lies.

They brought out a crock of winter berry ale. Torn took a little in his bowl. As did Sven. I declined. Not that I don't like winter berry ale — it's bitter and has bite, a splash in the bottom of a bowl is not enough to intoxicate. It warms the belly and soothes the mind.

But it was my mind and
   my belly and
      my belly was fine and
         so was my mind.

Below the confluence, the river flows flat to where the ice ends and the stones begin. In the valley the river follows one path. Out on the stony plain the river runs wherever it wants.

Torn remarked as we set out onto the field of stones, "It makes me happy not to be a Björkan enemy."

It wasn't the winter ale speaking. It was the stones — round boulders, wet and slippery. Walking was not easy. I tried to imagine an army marching across the stony plain — rocks and water and not a visible living thing for as far as any man could see. Yet they had come in years past, raiders who preferred to take rather than trade.

We met a man, a panner, late in the afternoon — nervous until he realized we didn't want his stones: his garnets, his rubies, his little bag of shiny pebbles.

We are Björkans, we have no need of things to decorate our fingers and our ears.

Nervous because the stony plain is a no man's land. Here, there is only one rule: If you kill someone, bury him.

The panner's camp was in a natural fortress between four large boulders. A humble bed beneath a rain shelter, a wooden box with straps for packing. He said his name was William. He offered us bread and water. But it was a bit too early yet for a Björkan to eat.

We stayed and listened to his stories — tomorrow stories — of days when he would be rich.

I felt pity for him, locked out of today. I gave him a story of a giant serpent that slithered among these stones. Its eggs were garnets and rubies and nuggets of gold. I told him that if he were to find the serpent's trail, it would lead him to the serpent's tail.

We made our own camp as the sun neared the flat

horizon on a gravel knoll only slightly higher than the rest of the stony plain.

Torn and Sven lit their sword hilts. I struggled with mine. Torn helped — shoved the tip of my sword deeper into the gravel, struck hard with his fire stone three solid cracks — and the wick embedded in the hilt flashed into flame.

We held our bowls filled with water over the sword flames until the water bubbled. I chose a button from my left sleeve, dropped it in the bowl, uncorked the spout to my hem pocket and shook out a spoonful of Navah to make the broth.

Three times we held our bowls over a flame the size of a finger; three times the broth boiled.

On the stony plain, there were no ice walls for the sun to flash upon. There were no ice walls to protect us.

We never spoke, but I am sure we each felt exposed as we held our bowls to the sky — as the sun dropped below the edge of the world, perfectly west, the night of the equinox.

Torn spoke what was in each of our thoughts. "He's putting down his staff."

I could see it if I allowed myself. The Winter Chief putting down the staff — the end of his term.

Whoever the women had chosen as Summer Chief would not raise her staff until the sun cleared the horizon tomorrow morning.

The celebrations would have just started in all the valleys of the Björkan. Tonight was the Night of Anarchy,

> a night of
>> feasting and
>>> dancing and
>>>> mating.

Some would drink more than a splash of winter berry ale. Most would eat a mushroom — or maybe two, if the fungi were small.

No sense in thinking of that; there was no one to dance with tonight, no one to mate with on the stony plain.

Sometimes people settled disputes violently on the Night of Anarchy. But Torrey had been a good Winter Chief; he knew instinctively where to find the agreement — that place between two disputants that each could reach. Tonight should be free of bloodshed.

The sound of rain on my bed roll woke me shortly before daybreak. I pulled the cover over my head and lay awake to listen, warm and dry beneath my björka robe.

When I next awoke, Sven and Torn were already rolling their bedding and tying it to their packs.

> We walked seven days,
>> seven buttons from our coats,
>>> seven spoonsful of Navah from our hems.

The mist began to lift by the zenith of the seventh day, and by early afternoon we could see the green hills on the stony plain's southern fringe. The rocks there were smaller and mixed with gravel. They moved beneath our feet but were better to walk on.

Torn seemed unscathed.

My shins were bleeding from falls.

Sven limped with a bad ankle.

At the very edge of the stony plain stood an expanse of water, maybe a hundred tree lengths across. On its opposite shore the forest began. Torn walked ahead confident. His warrior spirit carried him forward.

I followed — carefully, consciously — remembering the story of Stam and Matts. I looked back in time to see Sven sinking and went to help him. Maybe it was because of his bad ankle.

"Some people need to watch the reflection," I reminded him.

"It's not that. I always struggle with this," he answered.

We made it across with Torn and me on either side of Sven holding his elbows.

I spoke aloud the story of Stam and Matts as we crossed.

"The brothers:
    Stam the older,
        Matts the younger, and

their journey around the world
when it was new.
"They had walked
all the mountains, walked
all the valleys, walked
all the plains, and
seen it all
when it was small,
when the world still sparkled.
"They walked along the shore of a river and
the river became jealous of the brothers;
that they walked together and
enjoyed each other's company and
the river had to journey alone.
"In a moment when the brothers were not careful
while they were laughing,
the river reached up and grabbed Stam and
pulled him under and
drowned him.
"Matts had sat on the shore and
cried,
alone and afraid,
unable to continue, and
there was no going back.
There never is.
"In his grief,
Matts stuck his head

under the water,
    maybe to drown himself, but
        he didn't want to go alone and
        shouted for Stam.
"His older brother came to him and
  told him,
    'We can always walk together,
      younger brother.
        You walk on the surface and
        I will walk beneath and
          our feet will touch and
           I will hold you up and
            you will hold me down.'
"And that is why you should never laugh while you walk across water."

We took a break when we entered the forest. Crossing water takes even more energy — mental energy — than walking on slippery stones, and we all three needed a rest.

As we sat on our packs or with our backs against a tree, I wondered why Sven had trouble water-walking. He was a thinker; he should have a strong mind. He should be able to control his consciousness. But maybe his strength was also his weakness. The man could think, but to walk on water you also needed to believe.

THE TOWN

There were still a few hours of daylight remaining, so we pushed on into the forest. My feet were thankful for the soft ground — the fallen leaves and the mosses. Torn led, but it seemed he chose the densest bush to walk through.

I stopped and listened — reached out, searched around. "Hey Torn, there's a path toward our left."

I couldn't see it; I felt it strong.

"How far?" he asked.

"Ten tree lengths," I guessed.

It was there, but I had missed on the distance. It was closer to twelve tree lengths. By the time we were close, we all knew. The path we found was wide, rutted by carts. It ran generally in the direction we wanted to go — a bit toward the east from the due south of our travel.

I could smell the char before we came to the

clearing. They had chopped and burned the trees — either early in the winter or late autumn. They would be back soon to plant their grains around the charred stumps. I had heard the stories — but to see it,

> to see the death,
>> to see the scar,
>>> to see a forest
>>>> ripped and raw.

I lowered my head. Humans had done this — they weren't Björkan, but they were of our species. I felt shame. I spoke aloud my "sorry" and continued walking.

Sunset in a forest feels almost dismal — just a gradual dimming, no flash, no bursts of light. It's hard to know when to take a bowl of broth and meat. We made our camp well away from the smell of the charred clearing beneath a canopy of scented conifer boughs. A millennium of fallen needles softened the earth where we spread our bed rolls.

Torn said we should keep watches. Sven would take the first, Torn would take the middle, and I the morning. The middle watch is the hardest: sleep for three hours, stand watch for three, then try to fall asleep again for the last three.

No one gets more than six hours.

The morning watch is the best: wake before sunrise — be there when life begins to move, when the birds begin to sing, when the rodents climb back into the trees. I was watching not for enemies, not for trouble; I watched the world awaken.

Just before the zenith of the next day, we met two men carrying axes — iron axes with wooden hafts. They seemed surprised and looked as much at our clothes as at us. They stepped to the side of the trail to let us pass.

I looked at their faces and their hands — clean faces, grimy hands — before I looked at their clothing. They were dressed in a coarse material that I guessed was the woven hair of an animal. Wool — yes, wool. That was the word the story trader used to describe it. I had never seen it before; it made me glad for my björka silk.

These men wore no armour — they were not warriors; they were no threat to our passage. We passed. I nodded to them an acknowledgement. I acknowledged that they were human and that I saw them. We did not speak.

Torn picked up the pace, halfway between steady and swift.

Björkmen know four paces:
>
> sneak,
>> slow,
>>> steady, and
>>>> swift.

The further we travelled, the thinner the forest became, broken more and more by fields. By the time we reached the outskirts of a town, the forest was completely erased. I knew the name of the town from the story trader — Georgetown — and the river that flowed beside it they called the Spear.

I knew the story of George. He had been the left hand of a dominant warlord from further south. When the warlord died, his right hand replaced him and George fled north into the forest with a handful of supporters. They were the great-grandparents of most of the people there.

Stories and reality are different, or maybe it was just the story trader's lack of ability. I knew that town and its history — I knew the lineage of the people, I knew the structures and the functions. What the story missed was the dirt. When people are crammed behind walls and the forest is hewn into ramparts, the tree roots shrivel and loosen their hold. When the canopy no longer shades the ground, the mosses and lichens dry and die and there is nothing to hold the soil — to make it healthy — and the wind picks it up and tries to blow it back into the forest. When the rains come and turn the dirt to mud, the beasts and the carts splash it onto the buildings and onto the people.

The story trader also omitted to tell us about the smell. With the nearest forest a thousand tree lengths away, there was no place to defecate. My nose said they did their business in the street and it mixed with the mud that splattered the walls.

I stopped at the thought. I had nowhere to step. The story trader had spoken of their civilization, of their ability to grow crops, of their ale houses, of how they domesticated beasts to do their work for them. He had spoken of their music and their weaving. He had spoken at length of their ironworks — their forges and their shops.

But

    he had never mentioned

      the stink and

        the smell of

          rotted hides ready to tan, of

            the smoke from their fires and

            the feces in their streets.

It made sense now why he prized björka blossoms with their long-lasting scent. I wished I had one in my breast pocket to occasionally lower my nose to. I made myself a promise: at the very first stream we came to after we left Georgetown, I would stop and wash my feet.

The people at the alehouse knew the story trader: Anthony de Marchand. They said he had been there just after midwinter to buy boys. He had paid a good price and taken two. Probably gone to Stockade, maybe to Port.

I thought of the boys — sold by their parents — as we continued to journey southward. The purchaser didn't need chains to keep them; they were bound by their story. The story said they owed their parents a debt for the food they had eaten, for the roof that kept them dry, and for the blankets that kept them warm.

Sold to a merchant or
an army or
a miller or
an ironworker.
To buy a plow beast or
a cart beast that
could do more work than
a fourteen-year-old boy.

Five years of labour — it was a complicated story. It said they gave service and earned an education, and when they paid off the debt they owed to their parents by paying off the debt their parents owed to their buyer, then they would be free — owing nothing to no one — with the skills of an ironworker or miller or soldier or merchant. It was a powerful story of a duty owed that chained their minds so that no chains were needed upon their ankles.

Our journey — our story — continued southward along a well-travelled road. We often met a cart dragged by a beast. Some of the larger carts were dragged by two.

It was a land of rolling hills and deep, winding valleys. The forest there was mostly deciduous, speckled with meadows. Early blossoms were beginning to show roadside where we preferred to walk, rather than on the road itself. Grass and moss feel better under the feet than hardpacked gravel and grit.

The deforestation around Stockade was much greater than it had been around Georgetown. It began a full day's walk away and by mid-morning was complete. They had not left a single tree. Straight lines marked the fields — divided by pole fences to keep out the beasts.

Sven gave us warning; something was not right. He asked, "Where are the people?"

There were none, nor were there plow beasts. The fields were empty. "They should be planting by now or at least getting ready. Caution," he warned.

We heeded. Kept our pace at steady, paid attention.

We entered the stone walls of Stockade late after zenith — wandered from alehouse to alehouse asking if anyone knew Anthony de Marchand, the story trader.

Just before last light, when we were looking for a place to stay the night, by chance we met him. Or maybe not so much by chance, now that I think about it. Perhaps it was he who found us.

They came down the street pushing through the crowds: Anthony de Marchand and seven well-armed youths.

He smiled. "Björkans." He kept his hands down, his palms forward.

Sven was first to turn his palms forward — to greet in peace.

Torn held back,
hand on blade hilt,
eyeing the youths,
their blades and
spikes and
armour.
Caution.

"You've saved me a journey to fetch you. Imagine this — Björkans in Stockade. What a blessing. What an absolute blessing," said Anthony de Marchand.

He was clearly more than happy to see us. But there was something in his words that did not feel right. He wasn't lying. He knew better than that. He had come to the five valleys of the Björkan many winters to trade stories. Early on he had tried to trade false stories. He wanted Björkan blades, Björkan armour, and spools of woven Björkan silk. But a fancy made-up story about the deeds of a warlord only earned him trinkets. While a simple story of truth about the growing shortage of wild beasts or how the birds returned to the shore thicker than in years before would be paid for with a pile of goods from those in the circle who listened. Anthony de Marchand knew that any Björkan could tell if he failed to tell the truth. Truth words ring differently.

He chose his words carefully. "There are people here I would like you to meet."

His words rang almost true — but not quite. They sounded with an undertone of deceit.

Torn drew his blade.

"Wait." Anthony de Marchand held up his hands — palms toward us. "I think you will want to meet them too. They come from the stars."

I looked up.

Torn kept his eyes on the seven youths who were beginning to encircle us.

We were better armed than most of them. Those with iron armour could expect no protection from our Björkan blades. But a few of the older boys carried blades and wore armour we had traded for stories.

They were young and strong and bound by their duty owed.

We were Björkan,
    we were born knowing
        the ways of the warrior.
           It was in our blood and
              in our bones.
Our fathers and
    grandfathers and
        grandfathers before them
           had defended the five valleys;

                    their knowledge of blades and
                         armour and
                          arrows
              passed down enhanced to
                  the generations beneath them so
                     no Björkman needed to practise,
                        though some like Torn chose to
                         hone those skills until
                            the skill was as sharp as
                             a Björkan blade.

We were also taller and leaner, standing a full head above anyone near us. We are a slim people, but don't mistake that for weakness. Big muscles are often sluggish. We might have been born knowing the ways of the warrior, but we were taught grace and agility by our mothers and sisters.

We could have fought our way out of that mess — but then what? We were surrounded by Anthony de Marchand and his seven youths, who in response to Torn were beginning to draw their blades. If that had been all, we might have chosen differently.

But beyond the youths were hundreds, and beyond the hundreds were the stone walls of Stockade.

We could fight, but it would be long and bloody, and people would die who might not need to.

And all that was being asked of us was to meet some people who came from the stars.

"We will go." I spoke for us all. "But not as captives."

"My friends…" Anthony de Marchand spread his hands. "I have no wish to capture you. I only wish to introduce you to the aliens. I admit I am hoping for a benefit from the introduction. But maybe there is a benefit in it for you as well."

Those words rang true. I heard no tenor of a lie. I must admit, the thought of meeting aliens from the stars held a bit of intrigue for me. There was a story here. We had come to find out why Anthony de Marchand, the story trader, had not come to the valleys of the Björkan.

It seemed obvious.

It was because of the aliens.

THE ALIENS

The aliens were even shorter than Anthony de Marchand, though otherwise they didn't look much different from us: two arms, two legs, a head with a recognizable face.

Stockade had been built by a succession of warlords, each adding to the work of the previous until it became a sprawling mess. The aliens occupied the Hall of Shields as though they were holding court. Six of them on the dais — five males and a female. Too small on the chairs, their feet barely touched the floor.

I didn't understand their words, though I hear and speak all seven languages.

Anthony de Marchand spoke in reply, "They're Björkan, the ones you were looking for."

He indicated Sven, Torn, and I — a gesture with his right hand toward us, palm up, raised slightly at the end of the movement to indicate an elevated status.

To a Björkan

it was an act of scorn,

an insult.

We are equal people

none above another.

When we select our Winter Chief — before sunrise on the day following the autumnal equinox — men are sent to fetch him and drag him to his post. He fights back and sometimes is successful in winning his freedom and another needs to be chosen who doesn't fight as hard.

To indicate that any Björkan has a higher status is offensive. But it seemed to please the aliens. Three of the males stood and came toward us. One of them spoke to Anthony de Marchand.

He answered, "Björkans have powerful minds and abilities. There are not more than six or seven hundred of them in all their territory — yet no army has ever been able to conquer them. They control the weather and can bring storms against their enemies. They can change the earth and move the hills to make you lost. And some of them can fly. I know this; I have seen it with my own eyes."

Sven, Torn, and I were surprised — how could he have seen that?

When he had first begun to come among us, he had

asked to purchase a woman. The Winter Chief saved him — stopped us from killing him and being done with it. It was a mistake; the story trader was a human, and humans are allowed to make mistakes. But every Björkan woman learned of his mistake, and none would trade with him or talk to him or even acknowledge him after that. He didn't have any women's stories anyway.

So how could he have seen a Björkan fly?

The aliens spoke among themselves, and the female came toward me. She held a bone and bead choker with breast plate and offered to put it on me. She reached up but was too short. I bent down, lowered my head. She fastened it behind my neck.

The pain was instant.

I thought I had been tricked.

I thought I was going to die.

I worried that my ability to know the truth didn't work with aliens. I had trusted her because she gave no indication of malice. The pain only lasted about thirty heartbeats. When next the alien spoke, I understood his words. "Kind of a kick in the nuts the first time, ain't it?"

I understood the bone and bead choker with breast plate as well. All the aliens wore one.

Anthony de Marchand too wore a bone and bead choker — though without the breast bones and beads.

I put my fingers to mine. It was no different than

those our women sometimes made. Bone bead and silk string — more decorative than practical. It was called a breast plate but wasn't likely to stop an arrow.

"So you can move things with your mind? Show me," the alien said.

I sensed malice in his words and drew my blade.

"Hey Peter Pan with the wooden sword. Don't be fucken stupid." He drew a metal something from his waistband. "This is a forty-five-calibre Browning — it's the standard issue sidearm of the United States Army. It holds seven rounds, so I can shoot each of you fuckers twice and still have a bullet for this son-of-a-bitch if he is lying to me." He pointed the .45-calibre Browning at Anthony de Marchand.

Anthony de Marchand took half a step backward, his fear apparent. "I swear," he said. "I swear they can. But they are a stubborn people and you will have to persuade them."

"What persuades a Peter Pan?" The alien pointed the .45-calibre Browning at Sven.

"No — no — not like that." Anthony de Marchand stepped forward. "Force doesn't work with the Björkan. They will trade everything they have for a good story. Surely after travelling among the stars, you must have a few good stories for them."

"Where's the chaplain?" The alien turned to his kind. "Fetch the chaplain," he commanded.

When the chaplain came, he walked directly up to Torn, held something up, and shouted: "This is the Book of God. Kneel, you heathen, and be blessed by His words." He made to strike Torn on the forehead with the Book of God.

Torn knocked the Book of God out of the chaplain's hand with the flat of his blade. He could just as easily have taken the chaplain's hand but chose to be lenient.

Spit flew from the chaplain's mouth as he shouted, "He is a heathen and will not accept the Word of God. Dispatch him to Satan at once."

The alien with the .45-calibre Browning answered, "We need him — he might be a propeller."

The chaplain picked up the Book of God and shouted, "Sergeant John Marshall, are you afraid to meet God? We've travelled around this damned galaxy long enough. How many heathen worlds have we been to? A hundred?"

Sergeant John Marshall did not answer.

"If you think they are propellers, then take them to that damn bubble and give them to the witch."

"Chaplain, sir," Sergeant John Marshall controlled his tone. "I have God's work to do here. If you will let me at it."

"Get it done." The chaplain stopped shouting and walked away with the Book of God without looking back.

Sergeant John Marshall stood in front of Torn. "I should just fucken shoot you and be done with it. You have refused the Word of God — you have refused to redeem your soul. So now we will do things my way."

He pointed the .45-calibre Browning at Sven's knee.

There was an explosion and Sven fell to the ground. Blood poured from his knee and between his fingers as he held it.

Torn and I
    attacked as one.
        Another explosion and
           I saw Torn twisted.
           I saw Sven limping,
                bringing up his sword
                beside us.
                    Another explosion and
                    nothing.

Then I woke up here — on this pallet — in this forest. Then Lilly told me her story.

LILLY'S STORY

"We were seven women travelling together on the medicine trail. Our Ship Mother knew all the paths and places where medicine grew. She knew which planets were dead and which were alive. She knew water — live water and dead water. We landed on a planet to gather; one we had been to before. It was a place where the water was still alive, where the trees had memory and the rains still came to bless them — where mountains broke the wind.

"It was a planet with two and a half billion people — far too many already and more and more being born. They'd just had a war — a big war; they'd killed over fifty million. Mostly women and children.

"Their medicine lands keep shrinking,
        their cities keep expanding;
                smoke rises from billions of fires,

fills the sky,

fills the lungs,

fills the eyes.

No one cries.

"They are too busy digging the earth, clearing the forests. Even though they are ill — in body, mind, and spirit — they destroy their medicine places and kill their water.

"We knew to be careful. We had two guides — scouts — to watch and keep us safe.

"'Filthy stinking sasquatches,' Sergeant John Marshall called them after he shot them.

"We showed ourselves to save our friends — to doctor them. But the life had been smashed from their bodies. Medicine is life; it grows from living water. Medicine can enhance life, balance life. But when the life is gone, even the most potent medicines — the ones that grow from the original spores — cannot bring it back.

"We were captured in our grieving because we knelt beside the bodies of those scouts — those sasquatches — and howled our sadness. We sang their spirits back to the stars.

"They captured our Ship Mother first because she was the most visible, the most solid. They locked her hands behind her back, dragged her out of the valley, and carried the bodies of our friends.

"We followed.

"When they were forcing our Ship Mother into their machine, we came forward, showed ourselves. We couldn't let her be taken alone. We went into a machine with swirling blades above it that chopped the air and made the machine fly.

"We were taken to a place they called Fort Lewis. At first they were impossible to communicate with. Mother used her mind on the man called Colonel Mathew Sparks. She managed to entice him, first to examine a bone and bead choker, then she put the thought in his head that he should try it on.

"They are pirates — nothing more. They claim to be on a quest, that they are searching. But the place they seek does not exist — not in the way they imagine.

"They search the stars for
    their heaven, for
        their God, for
            a bearded old man
                on a golden throne
                    who drops manna with one hand
                    and
                        throws lightning bolts
                        with the other.

"And His son and angels with white wings playing harps and everyone lives forever — the way it is written in their book.

"We've taken them to over a hundred planets in this galaxy. Now they want to go to Andromeda. Maybe their God is hiding from them."

I had to ask, "What about Torn? What about Sven?"

"One of your companions was beyond medicine. The other recovers. You are the least injured. The bullet was slowed by your armour. Your left lung is broken but you breathe.

"Keep breathing

in — out,

in — out,

slow,

steady,

in — out.

"That's how to stay alive. Just keep breathing. The air in here is good — it's alive — but it's not your air. Your air is not this thick. Keep that bone and bead choker and breastplate on. The part that goes around your throat does your talking for you. The breastplate lets you breathe another planet's atmosphere.

"Breathe now.

Keep breathing.

It's going to be okay."

Which of my companions recovers and which was beyond medicine? Lilly didn't know their names. One was left on the floor where he fell; the other she brought here with me.

"Where is here?" I asked.

"You are on my vessel. They have hijacked it, but it is still my vessel. It goes nowhere without me."

"How did I get here?"

"I brought you."

"Why? What do you want with me?"

"They — not me. They want you. To propel this vessel, to help me push it to Andromeda. I told them I cannot do it alone."

Lilly put her palm on my chest. Raised it, then lowered it, drew up my breastbone, pulled in the air, then pushed down, pushed out the air.

"Steady,"
    she said.
        "In — out,
           keep breathing,
             keep breathing.
               That's how we stay alive."

I needed to know. Torn or Sven. Did I lose a brother or a thinker? "Take me to the other Björkan. Please," I begged.

Lilly denied me. "They won't allow it."

THE BUBBLE

"Will he live?" The chaplain looked down on me.

"He will live," Lilly answered.

"Can he push this ship?" a second alien asked.

"I have not fathomed his mind. But we are aware of the Björkan. We have gathered medicine in their five valleys. We know their women and their ways. The mind of the Björkan male is strong."

"Hear that, Bork," the second alien spoke. "You are an asset. But you can just as easily be a dead asset. This witch is going to show you how to be a propeller. Work with her and you will live long enough to see the Kingdom of God. If you refuse, we will give you to the sergeant, and you won't like his powers of persuasion."

The second alien dropped my blade beside the pallet I lay upon. "And you can keep your wooden sword. Now that you have learned not to bring a knife to a gunfight."

He turned to the chaplain. "Do you know what those buttons are made from? Did you hear what the trader said? He eats one of those a day with a spoonful of tree bark and that's all he needs. All we have to provide him with is a cup of water. One cup of water to boil his slice of snake meat and tree bark. Imagine if we could get our boys to live on those rations."

"Children of God do not partake in the meat of the serpent," the chaplain replied.

"To hell with that," the second alien laughed. "Most of our boys are from Louisiana — they grew up eating crayfish and alligator. They'd eat a snake if they could catch one."

He turned back to me. "There you go, Bork. You can burn your wooden sword to boil your snake meat. You and the witch can push this ship for us, and we will travel across the universe. Just play along and you'll have nothing to worry about. You got that, Bork?"

After a pause Lilly answered, "He gets that."

"That was Colonel Mathew Sparks," Lilly explained after they left. "He's the highest-ranking human here."

"Human?" I asked.

"It's the bone and bead choker," she explained. "We all call ourselves 'humans,' or that is the way it gets translated anyway. It's the same with our home planets. They all get translated as Earth."

I was three days upon the pallet — three days not

knowing which of my companions remained alive and which had gone back to the tree. But no, they would not have taken the body back to the five valleys and sat it under a björka tree. The birds and the insects would not carry his pieces and spread them on the earth. He would not have gone back into the soil and in turn be taken up by the roots of the björka and be brought up again through the stalk and out the branches into the canopy and be shown the sky and be released to the sky to begin the journey back to the stars.

No, in Stockade and in all the forts of all the warlords, they burn their dead without ceremony. They release the greasy smoke to the winds, trample the ashes into their streets — trodden by the hooves of cart beasts to be mixed with the mud and the manure. There the end of a man is much like the life of a man. No future. Merely mud, mire, and misery.

On the third day I arose — stood upon my feet — remembered Lilly's instructions and breathed

in — out,
   slow,
      steady;
in — out,
   slow,
      steady.

Stepped, stepped again, kept stepping, kept breathing.

Lilly said, "Breathing is the single greatest resistance to tyranny. Only when you have let out your last breath have you fully succumbed to the tyrant."

We went to see and found him lying on a pallet, his wounds still mending. He looked up at me as I approached.

"Torn, my love. Torn, my brother." I knelt beside his pallet and grasped his hand.

Then I wept for Sven, and Torn wept with me.

I told the story of Sven the best I knew. Born in the fifth valley of the Björkan. Raised up by the women his first seven years, taken by the men in a raid during the reign of a Winter Chief, taught the ways of men, taught that he should strive to understand. Before all things — understanding. Taught to guard the passageways into the valleys, that none would ever bring harm to the women and the girls and the boys under the age of seven.

I did not know Sven's kinship lines and could not tell them. I did not know his deeds, and I did not know what valour he had won. I told of his final journey and of the place where he fell. I wished him a continued story — where he would grow his understanding beyond these earthly dimensions and earthly tellings.

Then Torn and I said our farewell to Sven of the fifth valley of the Björkan. May he journey well.

Lilly led Torn and me out of the forest, walked

between us holding our hands. In the clearing, she looked up. Above us was a shimmering dome.

"That is the limit of our vessel. It's composed from living water," she explained.

"We're in a water bubble?" Torn sounded incredulous.

"Living water," Lilly corrected. "There's a difference. Living water connects to our life force — facilitates communication. It is part of the eternal vibration of the universe. Look," she said.

The light dimmed and we were able to see the stars through the bubble.

"There," she pointed. "That faint light. That's the Andromeda galaxy. It's twice the size of this galaxy and has a trillion stars. Colonel Mathew Sparks wants to go there."

I had to ask, "Why?"

"We've explored all of this galaxy — all the planets where we know life blossomed — searching for their heaven. It's not here. They think it must be deeper in the sky."

"How far?" I asked.

"Far," she answered. "Too far for me to push this vessel by myself. If my sisters were still with me, it would be easier."

"What happened to them?" Torn asked.

Even though Lilly was transparent and not very visible, I could see the sadness on her face.

"Sergeant John Marshall," she answered. She didn't need to say more.

The bubble contained a tiny world: a forest with a creek that rose up out of the ground near the edge, trickled over stones and ended at a waterfall that splashed into a pool.

She showed us the medicines in the forest. "This is Vera. She grows on a planet not far from your own. She takes away loneliness. I come to her often."

Lilly sat us on either side of the slender flowering plant. "Just sit," she said.

We sat and waited. Within seven heartbeats I saw the fifth valley of the Björkan, heard the wind in the björka leaves and the sound of children laughing.

Awash with sound and
   vision,
      warmth flowed through
        my core,
          filled me,
           fed me.
            I knew
             I was home.

"Come now. Vera is very powerful." Lilly offered us each a hand to help us stand. "She will seduce you, and when you have sat there long enough — without food, without water — you will succumb and let your life go. You will decompose and she will eat you. You are a bit large for her appetite. She prefers smaller animals. Offers them a gentle death."

We walked the forest path. "Medicine of the body and medicine of the mind. They grow together, work together. And here" — she pointed at the stream — "living water. Medicine for your soul."

THE ALIENS' CAMP

In sharp contrast to the forest, a line of tents, pegs driven into the earth. Trees felled — hewn into a barricade.

"The safety they create is far less than the safety they destroyed. Those trees would have protected them," Lilly whispered. "Shaded them, fed them, comforted them."

We stood together on the edge of the clearing, within the comfort of the trees, and looked out knowing there was no need to reshape or recreate their own world.

All they needed was to sit beside Vera for a moment.

"Do you know how to touch the mind of another?" Lilly asked.

It was a strange question — strange because I heard it in my mind. It made me smile.

"Now I do," I answered. "Now that I have felt it — yes, I can touch the mind of another."

"Here is the plan..." I heard her thoughts. "Colonel Mathew Sparks commands. He says yes and he says no. He stays stop and he says go. And what he says, the others do. If we touch his mind, shift his thinking, soften his fears, and strengthen his dreams, then maybe he will see that his world — the one they destroy — could be the heaven they seek."

I had a moral problem with this. Torn did not. Could I manipulate another? Take away their free will? Their power of choice? What right had I to do this?

Torn thought it was no different than moving the trail to make the enemy lost. The trail was where it always was. But when the men sat together and changed the story of the trail, our enemies could not find it. This would be no different than hiding the trail to their heaven from their commander — so thought Torn.

We laughed,
       not at the thought.
             It was a good thought.
                   We laughed because
                         we could hear
                               each other thinking. And
                                     Lilly laughed with us.

But Torn was wrong about the story of the trail. When the men sat together and changed the story, the trail did move.

Torn was a warrior; he would not know.

I am a storyteller and know to be careful — stories have power and can change the world.

THE JOURNEY

Torn and I stood the day watch; Lilly took the night. She changed the light in her vessel so it flashed at the simulated sunrise and again at sunset when Torn and I plucked a button and boiled our broth before our period of rest.

Together, we pushed the bubble vessel toward Andromeda. Nothing in the universe travels faster than thought. But Andromeda was far and our thoughts were limited — we were only human.

Lilly taught us how with pure thought.

I will try to explain with words. In the centre of the mind — the very centre — begins a tunnel that tapers away ahead of you. Go into the tunnel. Let yourself flow. At the end of the tunnel is an orifice that you must pass through. When you get to this point, you must be pure essence. When you squeeze through, you will be transformed into a beam.

Here you do not need to focus — you will *be* focused. You will be a line.

Point the line at Andromeda and let yourself go. You will be the thought and the thought will be you.

We propelled the bubble, but not because Sergeant John Marshall would shoot us if we did not. That was just death. We put our minds to the purpose because Lilly asked us to.

"Please," she said, "I cannot do this alone."

Beneath her words was a deeper purpose, something greater — more important than her and more important than us.

So we pushed by day and she pushed by night.

The aliens squabbled among themselves and Colonel Mathew Sparks was kept busy keeping order.

When we were not propellers, we reached out to his mind.

Gently,
    ever so gently,
        with thoughts and
            images and
                songs,
we showed him beauty and blessings and the reciprocity of kindness. We helped him experience his substance and its interaction with his essence. We touched his mind and his spirit, and when he came to visit, we touched his hands with ours.

On his world they do not lay hands palm to palm —
they grasp and pump. We learned to grasp and pump
his hand and smile and nod and listen.

Slowly,
　　day by day,
　　　slowly,
　　　　night by night,
　　　　slowly he
　　　　　began to see,
　　　　　　began to feel and
　　　　　　release his
　　　　　　hurt and
　　　　　　　heal his broken part.

When Sergeant John Marshall came to threaten or
to boast — to exercise his inner tyrant — we listened
politely, nodded, and waited. His commander was
coming and soon Sergeant John Marshall would be
ordered.

"The thing about tyrants," Lilly said, "is their love
of authority. They will kneel and grovel to any they
perceive above them, and stomp and spit upon any they
perceive beneath. They are forever trapped between
their tyrant and their tyranny — forever obeying and
demanding."

Of Sergeant John Marshall, she said, "Pity him. He
was sent to a war in a jungle — across an ocean far
away from his home, away from his mother. He saw

horrible things done to his friends, and his mind was injured — partly by what he saw, but mostly by what he was forced to do. It is for the things he has done that he cannot forgive himself. That is what makes him so mean. That is what makes him so weak. He is afraid that if he isn't angry and shouting, he will fall down and cry. So pity him and listen."

Sergeant John Marshall said, "I know that witch is lying. You are not pushing this ship with your minds. God never gave anyone that kind of power. There is a propulsion system here somewhere, and I am going to find it. And when I do, we will have no reason for that witch and you will all take a shortcut to hell."

We smiled and nodded. We understood. That was his way of saying he was too afraid to believe.

PERDITION BEGINS

Every seventh cycle of light, the chaplain, Captain Jesse Graham, broke the line of travel, interrupted the continuation of the thought. He demanded — commanded — that we attend a service behind the barricades that were not needed. Kneel and pray and sing and listen to Captain Jesse Graham preach.

"God the almighty,
    We know your work;
        we do your work.
            Bless us, Lord.
                Bless our endeavour.
"We waited, Lord.
    We waited and
        you did not come.
            We waited

one thousand nine hundred and
forty-seven years.
"We could wait no longer.
The forces of evil have taken over, Lord.
Satan walks the world unchallenged.
Bless our endeavour, Lord.
We pray
in Jesus' name,
Amen."

I listened to his words for the truth beneath them —
there was none. But there was no untruth either. They
were just words. We know that if a person believes an
untruth they will speak it as truth, and it will ring in our
ears as true. That was not the case with Captain Jesse
Graham, the chaplain. He neither believed nor disbe-
lieved the words he hurled at us.

They were just words,
pebbles to be thrown,
spoken for the sound they made
like the squawk of the skata bird,
who thinks its voice is beautiful
and
shrieks its song at all
who come near.

When the preaching and praying and singing of the
service was done, the aliens ate a feast.

"K-rations," said the corporal in charge of their food, as he held out a small rectangular box. "Eat and be damned grateful for what you get."

I heard Lilly whisper in my mind. "Don't eat it," she said. "You won't die if you do — but that food has no life left in it. It's dead in the package, and if you eat too many, you will be dead in your package.

"Life needs life," she taught. "Living water, living medicines, living foods. Those boxes they call K-rations hold substances that can be digested, but just because you can consume it doesn't mean it's good for you."

She sounded tired. She pushed the vessel alone during the dark period and was forced to listen to the chaplain when she should be resting.

I opened the K-ration and looked inside. There was too much for any Björkan man. I didn't need to count my buttons or weigh my hem. I knew the number and the weight. One sleeve was already empty and Andromeda galaxy was still far away, and somehow I had to make it home again.

I could maybe heat the can of beef and pork on my sword light — sear it, crisp it — maybe. But I didn't have to. Captain Jesse Graham said, "The Lord our God created the universe in six days, and on the seventh day he rested. Good Christians observe the sabbath and put aside our labours. But you are heathens: the rules do not apply to you. So get your arses back to that tree you like so much and let's get moving again."

The tree we liked so much was a björka that Lilly and her sisters grew.

I wondered at Lilly's age. She said she had been present at the planting, witnessed a seedling become a tree. And the tree she witnessed became as large as any in the five valleys. Either trees grew faster here or Lilly aged slowly.

Torn and I sat beneath her branches, found the place in our minds, found the tunnel, flowed through the orifice, sought Andromeda in the distance and poured ourselves in its direction.

Colonel Mathew Sparks came to visit, to sit beneath the branches with us.

He spoke of his home
    in a place he
        called Oregon.
            Of forests and
                mountains and
                  oceans and
                  weather.
                Of a sister,
                  a brother, and
                    one time,
                      a mother.

His mind became gentle. We listened to him remember. He told us of the day of his mother's passing. He'd been in the field, in a horror place he called

Guadalcanal. He had gone alone to the shore where none would see and screamed into the dark at the water and took out his pistol and tried to kill the water because he blamed it, because that morning he had seen her face on its surface.

"Was that crazy?" he asked. What did we think?

We thought it was perfectly normal for a mother to come visit her son and show him her face on the water before she began her journey. But yes, it was crazy to blame the ocean and try to kill it for bearing the message and showing the image.

His mind stirred.

I sent good thoughts in that direction, but they were partially blocked by his sorrow. Sadness rose up in him — brought on by the memory of his mother. He struggled to hold it down.

I whispered in his mind a soothing sound and gave him back the image
        of a place he called Oregon,
              of forests and
                    mountains and
                       oceans and
                          weather.
                    Of a sister,
                       a brother, and
                          one time,
                             a mother.

The sorrow surged within him — broke free and poured out of his being. He opened his mouth and the sorrow spilled out in a whimpering sound. It came out of his eyes and his nose and even through his skin. He had held it so long — it needed to go and it oozed out of his pores.

The earth beneath the björka tree absorbed Colonel Mathew Sparks's tears and snot and spittle drip. The earth took the water and took the sorrow and kept it.

In that moment I witnessed my understanding grow. Sorrow is flushed from the body with water, and water is alive when it holds emotions.

It was the memory of his mother that began the deluge. But he cried to his father. "Father, forgive me — forgive me, please. They said the Japanese would never surrender. So I never let them. My men made necklaces from their finger bones. They polished skulls and sent them home."

He went to his knees. "Father, forgive me. I cut off their ears to dry in the sun. My collection — my collection. Father, forgive me. Forgive us all. Forgive us our sins —"

"What the fuck is this?" Sergeant John Marshall yelled. He grabbed his .45-calibre Browning and pointed it at me. "Did you do this?"

I wondered: *Was I responsible? Or was Colonel Mathew Sparks's mother responsible?*

"It wasn't us." I spoke the truth. "He needed to heal and we helped him."

"Sir," Sergeant John Marshall offered a hand.

Colonel Mathew Sparks struggled to stand.

"You had better come with me, sir."

THE COURT MARTIAL

Colonel Mathew Sparks stood,
    stared straight ahead,
        his hands fastened behind him.
            Chaplain Captain Jesse Graham held court.
Sergeant John Marshall gave evidence. "I was measuring our progress, sir. We have been travelling at about fifty thousand times the speed of light when the witch is the propeller. During the day, when these two are propelling, we move considerably slower — about thirty-five thousand times the speed of light. We'd started to move again after this morning's service, sir — then we came to a stop. I went to discover the problem. When I found them, the colonel was kneeling on the ground at their feet. He was in a disgraceful situation — crying and sobbing. I believe, sir, that the colonel is no longer fit to command."

"Do you have anything to say in your defence?" Chaplain Captain Jesse Graham asked.

Colonel Mathew Sparks continued to stare straight ahead. He did not answer.

"In that case, I have no option but to relieve you of your command. Sergeant Marshall, I order you to dispatch the colonel at your discretion."

A few moments later, we heard the explosion from the .45-calibre Browning.

Then there were only seventeen hijackers remaining in Lilly's vessel.

PERDITION

In the days that followed, we heard more explosions from .45-calibre Brownings. The hijackers smelled of fear — first of each other, then of everything around them. A guard was posted to protect us.

Corporal Timothy Shanks, with
a rifle slung on
his shoulder and
an anger that
ate at
his soul.

His mind was untouchable, filled with hate and despair — no good thoughts could penetrate. There was no kindness there. He kept his back to the björka, constantly ready to fight.

A body can do that for just so long before it begins

to consume itself. A mind can stay in battle, but a spirit needs its rest.

We witnessed his conflict and watched Shanks tear himself apart. He began to curse for no reason — spit anger in words to his God. "Where the fuck are you hiding?" he swore up toward the dome.

He crouched with his rifle pointing. "What would happen, I wonder, if I put a hole in that fucken bubble?"

"Probably nothing," I answered. "It's a life you cannot take with a gun."

"What the fuck do you know? Fucken Peter Pans. I'm with the sergeant — you bastards aren't pushing us with your minds. There's a propulsion system somewhere, and when we find it, you won't be needed anymore."

I heard Lilly whisper, "Don't engage. Keep your mind on Andromeda, please. I need your help. Remember."

We ignored Corporal Shanks when he said, "I started killing Japs when I was eighteen. Now it's easy."

When Lilly made the light bounce inside the bubble — the way it does at sunset in the fifth valley of the Björkan — Torn and I withdrew our minds from the quest for Andromeda, pushed the tips of our blades into the soil, and lit the hilts. We boiled our meat and broth three times, said our thanks to the heavens — to the essence — spilled a drop on the ground for the substance, and supped in silence.

It had been at least seventy buttons since we last

spoke to each other with words, since Lilly taught us to talk with our thoughts. Then, more than ever — when the hijackers were killing each other — words that could be heard were dangerous.

"If they keep at it," Torn's thought sounded happy, "pretty soon there won't be any of them left."

I wondered if Lilly was listening. She didn't respond when that thought went out, so I assumed she wasn't.

"I have a problem, my brother." I sent a thought to Torn.

"What is it?" he replied.

"My problem is with Lilly. We both know she is telling the truth — she needs us to push this vessel. But there is something she is not telling, something more, something beneath."

"I sensed it too," Torn thought back. "She tells the truth but not all of it — there is something else. She becomes very uncomfortable when anyone mentions searching this vessel."

Was that the truth? I needed to examine. Were those our thoughts, or were we being caught up in the distrust and hatred around us?

We could be mistaken.

"Torn, do you trust me?" I asked.

"Yes, I do, brother," he replied. "But you are the only one I trust completely."

And I knew I trusted Torn. So it wasn't us.

"Lilly," I shouted in my mind. "Lilly, can you hear me?"

"I hear you, Juha," she answered. "I hear you fine. How can I help you, my Björkan friend?"

"Lilly, my friend, we have a question: What are you worried Sergeant John Marshall is going to find?"

My question was answered with silence — a long, uncomfortable silence. I reached to seek out her mind. But my reaching was parried and stopped.

"I need your help to propel this vessel." Lilly's thought was a whisper. "But the help I need is not for myself. There are five little ones hiding."

Then I heard them — children's voices.

I remembered before I was seven — before the raid in the night when the men came to take me — children playing and laughing.

Torn must have heard them too, must have remembered before he was seven.

"Come, brother." His thought was a shout. "We need to defend this valley."

Two quick strides and a slash with his blade and Corporal Timothy Shanks lay dying, splashing his blood on the ground.

"Oh no,

 oh no."

  I heard Lilly's whimper.

   "This vessel cannot absorb

    any more killing."

"Tell the children to hide their eyes," Torn spoke aloud. "Come, brother, draw your blade. There is no one else; it's up to us."

He began to stride swiftly in the direction of the barricade. I drew my blade and followed.

"For Sven," Torn said

　　　as he killed the first man.

　　　　　"For the children,"

　　　　　　　he said when he killed the second.

"Wait," screamed Lilly behind us.

　　　"Wait, don't be doing this."

But Torn wasn't listening — his warrior was too strong within him. If only he hadn't heard the children. He fell when the bullet hit him. The vessel went completely dark when Lilly shut off the light.

THE DARK AGES

I crawled in the dark toward Torn. The only light came from the flashes from the hijacker's weapons.

The vessel was filled with a loud
   crack!
     crack!
       crack!
        and the sound of
          men shouting.

I found Torn and wrapped my arms around him. I had time. It had been less than a hundred heartbeats. I told the story of the last few moments — how Torn's warrior spirit had awoken when he heard the voices of the children, how he had slain Corporal Timothy Shanks, then attacked the barricades. I told of his killing the first two enemies he met. Then Lilly shut off the lights and Torn and I lay down to avoid the bullets flying.

He stirred in my arms and I told him, "I changed the story of your attack. In the old story you were killed."

As Torn and I crawled back into the forest, one of the hijackers fired a bright light into the sky. From then on there were no more days. Lilly kept the vessel in perpetual night. She decreed:

"There will be no more killing,

not in front of the little ones,

not in front of the medicines.

No more killing,

no more madness.

You and your brother must stop.

I will hide you.

I will protect you.

But the killing must

come to an end."

From then on, Torn and I hid in the forest. We could have ambushed them a hundred times — slit their throats in the dark, slid a blade through their rib cages. Björka wood through their hearts.

Torn and I kept our word: we killed no more.

But the hijackers had made no promise. They kept a fire behind their barricade and killed more trees to keep it burning. They sent out patrols to find us, carrying flaming torches made from broken branches.

Lilly cried every time a tree fell, and the children whimpered in the dark.

"Lilly," I said. "We cannot continue like this. You said it was you who moved us from the planet to this vessel. Can you transport the hijackers somewhere else?"

"It doesn't work like that," she answered. "I connect the life force of this vessel to the life force of the planet and merely facilitate the passage along the corridor."

"So, if we come close to a planet, you can send them off?"

"Still no," she answered. "They must want to go."

"But I didn't want to come here, and you brought me."

"You were unconscious and couldn't resist."

"What if we knock them all out?" Torn suggested.

"No more violence," Lilly answered. "This vessel is a sacred place. It has been defiled enough."

"It's them doing the defiling," I argued. "It's them cutting the trees. It's them trying to kill us. You must know a medicine that will put them to sleep and then you can put them off."

"Yes, there are medicines that would put them to sleep. But how would we get them to drink it? And even if we did get them to drink the medicine, there are no living planets nearby. We are two-thirds of the way to Andromeda. There are a few dead rocks out there, but they have no life force to connect to. This vessel has been weakened by the killing. Its life force might not be strong enough to open a corridor. I am sorry to offer such little hope. It was I who put Andromeda in their minds. I thought if we took them to Andromeda — if they saw my home planet, if they experienced all our love and kindness — they would think they had found their heaven.

"But now,

now that I have seen what they have done,

now that I have seen what they can do,

I don't want to take them there

anymore."

We hid in the dark — avoided their patrols, cupped our hands around our sword lights when we boiled our meat and our broth.

Lilly and the children were safe for the time being. They were already translucent and hard to see. In the dark they were completely invisible. Only Torn and I needed to hide.

I tried to negotiate. I shouted from the edge of the forest, "Captain Jesse Graham. We need to talk."

My words were answered with bullets and shouting. Then the voice of the chaplain, Captain Jesse Graham: "Here's the deal. It's the only deal I will give you. You and your brother surrender. Submit to punishment for the murders you committed, and the witch takes us the rest of the way to Andromeda. I am not about to bargain with murderers."

EZEKIEL

The only way to get them off the vessel was if they
wanted to go — so, where did they want to go? They
wanted to meet their creator — their judge. They
needed to be forgiven. They had two ways to get there.
They could die good Christians and their souls would
make the journey, or they could hijack a spaceship and
search the width of the universe looking for their heav-
enly Father.

    Then I remembered a story.

        Chaplain Captain

          Jesse Graham.

            His mouth all froth and spittle,

              a sermon

                on the morning

                  of a seventh day.

      He had shouted: "This is the ship of a witch, Lord.

Forgive us. We come to you in this blasphemous bubble. And that is why you hide the way from us. Send to us, Lord. Please send to us the wonderous spaceship you sent to your servant Ezekiel."

"Hey Lilly, hey Torn, do you remember a sermon about a spaceship?"

"Yes," Torn answered.

"Yes," Lilly laughed. "Come," she said. "Tell that story, Juha. Come to the edge of the vessel and tell that story to out there."

"I will need help." I, too, felt about to laugh. "It's a big story to tell. I can't tell it by myself."

"Okay — but I don't get it," Torn answered.

"You will," Lilly laughed as she led.

We sat at
    the edge of
      the vessel,
        close against
          the bubble and
            told the story from
           the sermon,
             told it out into
              the void.

"And I looked, and, behold a whirlwind came out of the north, a great cloud, and a fire infolding itself, and a brightness was about it, and out of the midst thereof as the colour of amber, out of the midst of the fire.

"Also out of the midst thereof came the likeness of four living creatures. And this was their appearance; they had the likeness of a man.

"And every one had four faces, and every one had four wings.

"And their feet were straight feet; and the sole of their feet was like the sole of a calf's foot: and they sparkled like the colour of burnished brass.

"And they had the hands of a man under their wings on their four sides; and they four had their faces and their wings.

"Their wings were joined one to another; they turned not when they went; they went every one straight forward.

"As for the likeness of their faces, they four had the face of a man, and the face of a lion, on the right side: and they four had the face of an ox on the left side; they four also had the face of an eagle.

"Thus were their faces: and their wings were stretched upward; two wings of every one were joined one to another, and two covered their bodies.

"And they went every one straight forward: whither the spirit was to go, they went; and they turned not when they went.

"As for the likeness of the living creatures, their appearance was like burning coals of fire, and like the appearance of lamps: it went up and down among the living creatures; and the fire was bright, and out of the fire went forth lightning.

"And the living creatures ran and returned as the appearance of a flash of lightning.

"Now as I beheld the living creatures, behold one wheel upon the earth by the living creatures, with his four faces.

"The appearance of the wheels and their work was like unto the colour of a beryl: and they four had one likeness: and their appearance and their work was as it were a wheel in the middle of a wheel.

"When they went, they went upon their four sides: and they turned not when they went.

"As for their rings, they were so high that they were dreadful; and their rings were full of eyes round about them four.

"And when the living creatures went, the wheels went by them: and when the living creatures were lifted up from the earth, the wheels were lifted up.

"Whithersoever the spirit was to go, they went, thither was their spirit to go; and the wheels were lifted up over against them: for the spirit of the living creature was in the wheels.

"When those went, these went; and when those stood, these stood; and when those were lifted up from the earth, the wheels were lifted up over against them: for the spirit of the living creature was in the wheels.

"And the likeness of the firmament upon the heads of the living creature was as the colour of the terrible crystal, stretched forth over their heads above.

"And under the firmament were their wings straight, the one toward the other: every one had two, which covered on this side, and every one had two, which covered on that side, their bodies.

"And when they went, I heard the noise of their wings, like the noise of great waters, as the voice of the Almighty, the voice of speech, as the noise of an host: when they stood, they let down their wings.

"And there was a voice from the firmament that was over their heads, when they stood, and had let down their wings.

"And above the firmament that was over their heads was the likeness of a throne, as the appearance of a sapphire stone: and upon the likeness of the throne was the likeness as the appearance of a man above upon it.

"And I saw as the colour of amber, as the appearance of fire round about within it, from the appearance of his loins even upward, and from the appearance of his loins even downward, I saw as it were the appearance of fire, and it had brightness round about.

"As the appearance of the bow that is in the cloud in the day of rain, so was the appearance of the brightness round about. This was the appearance of the likeness of the glory of the Lord. And when I saw it, I fell upon my face and I heard a voice of one that spake."

Torn and I are Björkan: we hear a story once and we can repeat it. So too could Lilly, we discovered.

When we finished telling the story from Chaplain Captain Jesse Graham's sermon,

the story became.

Ezekiel's spaceship became.

Its lights became and

its spinning wheels became.

We needn't have worried about the hijackers' willingness to be transported. They begged Lilly to go and she sent them.

COMPATIBILITY

When the hijackers were gone, Lilly turned on the lights again. Torn and I helped her and the children to heal the damage done to their vessel. We tore apart the barricades and spread the logs in the forest.

"This is mycelia," Lilly taught. "It is the communication system of the forest." She spread a handful upon a log on the ground. "It will eat the dead wood — turn it back to life."

She touched the sleeve of my coat. "This too is mycelia," she said. "Your women collect it from the björka tree and weave it."

I did not know that. I had always thought björka silk grew from the tree.

"No, they live together. The silk and the tree need each other."

As we worked, Lilly told stories. "On all the planets

in all the galaxies, there is life, because life is part of the universe. Life needs the universe and the universe needs life — the same way that the mycelia needs the tree and the tree needs the mycelia. Everywhere there is life, it looks the same. You and I each have two arms and two legs, a head and a torso. And as you saw, so, too, did the hijackers. On every planet where life took hold, you will find people with two arms and two legs, a head and a torso.

"The rules of the universe are simple. Life repeats itself everywhere the same because it follows those simple rules. If you look out a long distance, you will see that the universe — made up of billions of galaxies — looks like mycelia. If you look inside your brain, again you will find structures that look like mycelia. If you look inside your heart, you will find in the muscles a similar structure.

"The first life to take hold on any planet is always the mycelia — it fruits into fungi and feeds upon the planet and

    feeds the planet

        until the planet

            is strong enough to

                support the plants and

                    then the animals."

This was a woman's story — or maybe it wasn't; maybe it was a universe story.

I looked at Lilly and tried to see her — tried not to see through her. I realized she wore no clothes.

"What are you staring at?" Lilly smiled at me.

I had been staring at her groin.

"We are compatible — we can mate. If that is what you are wondering."

"No,

no."

I denied it.

"I was just trying to see."

Lilly walked away a few steps, looked around on the ground, and picked at a tiny flower. She pulled three petals from it and ate them one at a time. Her translucence diminished. I was able to see her more clearly — she became the purplish colour of the flower petals.

"Is this better?" she asked, standing beautifully naked in front of me.

I cannot deny — I am a man — I felt the attraction, a surge in my masculinity. I did not need to answer, not with words; my thoughts were strong.

Lilly responded with thoughts of her own. She raised her arms toward the treetops, spread her feet a little wider, tilted her head back, thrust out her pelvis, and began to sing.

Her voice was the sound of
wind on leaves of

                    water over stones of
                          birds and
                        insects' wings
                      hovering over a
                       pollen-laden
                          flower.

The song drew me to her. It filled my mind until
there were no thoughts that were my own; it filled my
body until I was only a tingle of nerve endings. Her
body filled my eyes. My mouth felt empty and thirsty —
my heart felt strong and sure. I felt my need, and Lilly's
song said I was needed.

HOMEGOING

We lay on the soft earth of a forest floor,
   wrapped in arms and legs,
      holding dear and
         never wanting to leave,
            never wanting the moment
            to end, to
               stretch in infinity to
                  the other end of the universe
              and
                 back again.

"We have to figure out how to send you home, my love," Lilly whispered in my ear.

But I didn't want to go; I wanted to stay.

"No," Lilly continued to whisper. "I must take the little ones home. It's not far from here. I can do it alone.

But you, my beauty, you must go home, and Torn too. Your people wait for you."

I knew what she said was true. There were only two buttons remaining — my coat was almost empty.

But home was a long way away, and my heart and my mind and my body had been enraptured.

"The problem is," Lilly continued, "this vessel has been weakened, and the planet with the five valleys of the Björkan is very far away. I cannot connect the life force of this vessel with the life force of your planet with sufficient strength to send you and Torn home."

If it had just been me, I would have stayed. But Torn needed to go home and, truth be told, I knew I could not stay.

Lilly and I were compatible, and I wanted to seek her out on every Night of Anarchy and every day in between and mate and make babies and create new stories. But my story and her story were separate and needed to be told on our own planets.

I agreed — reluctantly — that Torn and I needed to go home.

I told Lilly the story my mother Ingra told me — about the connection between Substance and Essence.

As I told it, the effects of the flower petals began to weaken and Lilly slowly became less visible, and I realized she was more essence than substance.

Her essence,
  my substance
    joined in
      lovemaking.
        The energy,
          the new something
          that resulted
            was what she used
              to send me and Torn
              home.

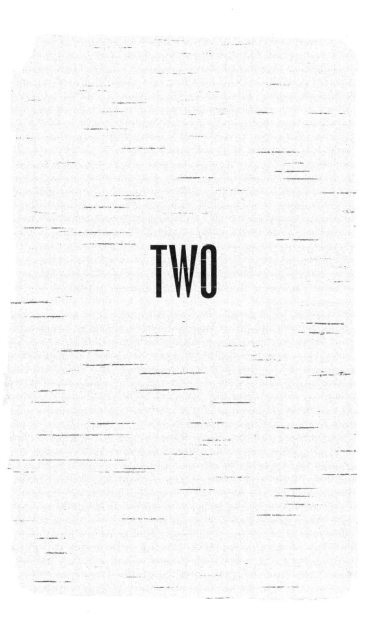

TWO

HOMECOMING

Whatever our lovemaking created — our tiny force in the universe — whatever remained must have stayed with Lilly or somewhere between. It did not come home with me.

Torn and I arrived two days before the Summer Chief put down her staff. Away an entire season, away an entire galaxy, and found a way home — home to kneel beneath a björka and mourn, to speak the words of sending Sven to the stars.

"Björka, Brother Mother Sister Father," Torn and I spoke in unison. "Take up our brother Sven. Take him up from the ashes left on the stones of Stockade. Take up his spirit with your roots — take him up through your mighty stalk. Release him through your leaves. Release him toward the sky. Let him begin his journey home — his journey back to the stars."

We had nothing of his to leave, to place upon the ground. Instead, we left our tears to soak into the earth and moisten the björka's roots.

My abode welcomed me home — the door opened when I approached. I sat first upon the step and looked the length of the fifth valley of the Björkan — looked long, looked with awe, looked with love, and let my being be. I let my essence merge with the substance of my home, let my substance merge with the essence of my valley.

We gathered when the time came to accept the equinox — the people of the fifth valley of the Björkan, like all the people in all the valleys — as the Summer Chief put down her staff, as the sun set, as the night came.

I had no plan
    except to be,
        except to experience
            this Night of Anarchy,
                this night of abandon,
                    this night of music,
                        this night of love,
                            this night of joy.

Chief Asa's staff touched the earth — was laid flat for a second or three, still amid the cheer, the singular shout from a hundred throats — when I was tackled from behind and thrown to the ground. I rolled onto my back and was sat upon. Freja straddled me, held me by my wrists, tilted back her head, and laughed up toward the sky. And then she brought down her face — brought down her mouth to mine — to kiss me with more than passion, more than the greed of need. She pushed her spirit into me and filled my mouth and my throat and my mind.

My body awoke and responded, surged with love of my own.

Freja shed her garment and stripped me of mine — straddled me again, took me into herself, and howled her pleasure at the sky. She added her voice to the howls and shrieks of the hundreds around us — all screaming, all cheering, all enjoying, and many enjoining.

We gave love
    back and forth.
      We gave love,
        we took love,
          we shared love.
            We tasted and
              we voiced love.

We filled our senses with each other — our eyes and our mouths and our hands and our skin. Again and again, and in between, we danced or joined a circle and sang. Freja had brought a jug of strong winter berry ale. We shared. I sipped from her bowl and she sipped from mine.

The intoxication from the liquor was minor compared to the intoxication I obtained from the power and essence and substance and joy of Freja — her body and her mouth and her mind and her heart and her soul. And because she gave me those things so freely, I gave back my body, my mouth, my mind, my heart, and my soul.

Again and again — past the night zenith on toward the dawn — dancing, singing, enjoining. We merged essence and substance — mouth met mouth, skin met skin.

Voice with voice in song.

Heartbeat to drumbeat,

a rhythm of feet,

a dance toward dawn and

on and

on.

Swaying our bodies to the music of flute and drum and strum — among the hundreds around us — being Juha and being Freja and being Björkan among the people of the björka tree. Being in the fifth valley: being of the people — being of the people — being of the people. The thought resonated, repeated itself. A drum beat in my mind. I, Juha, of the people, of the people. I am one with Freja. I am one with the people.

As the light came, we lay entangled, spent arms and spent legs and spent torsos — satisfied hearts, sanguine minds, and sublime souls.

DUTY ACCEPTED

"I must be getting up soon, my dear," I whispered toward Freja's ear.

"Why, why must you? The Winter Chief will not raise his staff until after the sun has risen," she answered.

"Because, my dear, I am one of the ones who will fetch the next Winter Chief and drag him to the chair."

"Who has been selected?" Freja shifted in my arms.

"We will grab Torn." I laughed at the thought.

Poor, unsuspecting Torn. He did not know we had arranged among the men to grab him just before the sun rose. It was our brother Åke who came to me with the idea, who came to me with the plan and said it had been agreed. Did I agree? Would I assist in the grabbing of Torn and the forcing of him to the chair? I agreed.

The light was getting brighter. I really needed to leave — but the warmth of Freja, the love of Freja — but I really needed to leave.

"I must —" I began.

Her mouth on mine swallowed my words.

"Once more. Just once more." She rose and straddled me.

I looked at the light. I really should be going. But she had me and was riding me slow — her back arched, her eyes toward the sky.

If I was a few minutes late in the grabbing of Torn, what difference would it make?

I closed my eyes to the image of Freja above me — her body and her breasts and her throat and her hair falling and her face and her eyes.

I felt her hands upon my wrists pinning my arms above my head, as she rode me harder and harder. We joined in our release — in our letting go, in our thrusting and throbbing.

Then I felt hands on my ankles and opened my eyes.

Freja stood above me laughing. "Let me be the first to congratulate you on being selected as the next Winter Chief," she said as she stood and reached for her garment, still hanging from the bough of the björka tree.

Torn laughed. "Got you."

Those were his hands upon my wrists.

There were more than a dozen of them come to grab me. In the melee that followed, I twisted and kicked and cursed to no avail. Outnumbered, outmuscled, set up and ambushed.

Set up. There was Åke. Åke my brother — my co-conspirator to drag Torn to the chair — held my right arm, and Torn held my left.

I had been so easily fooled because I wanted to be fooled. I wanted to believe that the men had chosen Torn. And Freja — she must have known, must have agreed to keep me occupied.

It would not have been so bad if Torn had not been laughing so loud.

But brother, it is not he who laughs the loudest. It is he who laughs last.

I relaxed my right arm until Åke did not hold it so tight, then yanked it free — twisted my body as I swung a fist up into Torn's face. I caught him in the mouth. My knuckles split his lip. He spit blood before he cursed.

I laughed loud in his face.

He cracked me back beneath my left arm. That rib was going to hurt for a few days. I laughed anyway. I pulled my right arm away from Åke again, but let him hold on and struggle to pull it back. Then I shoved it back with him pulling on it — caught him in the solar plexus with an elbow, stole his wind, dropped him to his knees, gasping and cursing.

Then Torn took charge. He told the men to put me on the ground and roll me onto my stomach. When they picked me up again, they carried me face down. I could kick and twist and struggle, but I could not see my targets.

By the time we arrived at the abode of the Winter Chief, there were nearly a hundred men shouting and cheering. They stood me up, turned my back to the abode. I was not done yet.

Until my ass was in the chair,

I was not the Winter Chief.

I surged with renewed strength. I fought with my all, but my all was not enough. I was put in the chair. The men let me go. I sat, looked down and took a breath — then raised my head and nodded my acceptance.

Then Torn announced, "Juha Torrey's son of the fifth valley of the people of the Björka: You have been chosen by the men of this valley to be our Winter Chief. Are there any here who disapprove?"

"None," rose the shout from all the men.

Torn continued, "The duty put upon you is to serve to the best of your ability — to the best of your intelligence, to the best of your strength, to the best of your being — all the people of this valley. Remember the children and the women first in your decisions. Remember the björka tree and be strong."

I stood. No words of acceptance were needed. It

was understood that the duty had been put upon me. I had fought and lost. I would be the Winter Chief. I would serve for two hundred and five days until the next equinox.

Torn turned to a young man named Magnus. "Where is his staff?"

Magnus replied, "I went to his abode and searched. I could not find one."

"I have never made a staff," I confessed.

"Well, how are you supposed to raise your staff and end the Night of Anarchy if you don't own one?" Torn shouted to the gathered crowd, "Does any here have a staff to give the next Winter Chief?"

An odd request. Once a man has made his staff, it is his for life — no one has a spare or one to share.

Freja came forward — a long slender wand in her hand. "If I may?"

"You may." Torn took the slender staff and put it in my hand.

JUHA'S TENURE

Thus my tenure as Winter Chief began when I raised a woman's staff, and order and decorum returned to the fifth valley of the Björkan as the sun came over the East Wall. Normally, once the staff of a new chief has been raised — be it a man's or a woman's — everyone goes to bed and sleeps at least until the sun reaches its zenith.

But not this time. A delegation of women petitioned me immediately. Asa the past Summer Chief, Ingra my mother, Signe the oldest woman in the fifth valley, and Freja. It had just been put upon me to consider the children and women first in all my decisions.

I accepted the petition.

Once we were all in my new abode, Freja closed the door and put her back to it. Asa, Ingra, and Signe each crossed their feet and sat on the floor. I would have preferred to join them there, but I was now a Chief and a Chief sat in a chair.

Asa spoke first. "During my tenure as Summer Chief I sent scouts into the world to bring back the news."

How? I wondered. The valley would be closed by the rush of the river through the chasm.

"The news that came back was not good, and you need to know it immediately."

I nodded and waited.

Asa continued, "It seems Anthony de Marchand has got his hands on some weapons." She turned to look at Freja.

Freja finished Asa's thought: "And he is coming this way with an army."

"If the weapons came from the aliens," I guessed — because there was nowhere else they could have come from — "he can't have more than one or two. He might have a forty-five-calibre Browning. Maybe a rifle. I don't think they would have given him a machine gun."

Freja reported: "His first attack was on the iron-works at Mora."

Oh damn, I thought. The Mora Ironworks was where the true artisans of metallurgy lived and worked. They added carbon to their iron, which made it almost as strong as hardened björka wood. "But still," I said, "even if Marchand can convince the Morans to manufacture firearms, guns alone are not a threat to us. He needs ammunition to go into the guns."

Freja answered with two words: "Dragon Blood."

I inhaled. So that was why he was on the march here. I let out my breath.

I did not speak,
    there was no need.
      We all knew,
        we all could see.

The björka tree grew elsewhere beyond the five valleys, but only rarely. And when it did, they didn't wait for it to mature — to grow old and begin to lean, to pull back its roots until nothing held it to the earth before it fell.

In the five valleys, when a björka falls we see a sacrifice — a blessing — to the people: homes and bowls and spoons, armour and blades and arrows and bows and spears, tools and utensils and shoes.

In the outer world, to find a björka tree meant immediate wealth. They hacked it as soon as they found it, sold or traded the wood while it was still wet and malleable, while it could be carved and shaped before hardening.

And sometimes — once in a great many trees — the heart of the björka runs red with Dragon Blood.

I asked, "How much do we have?"

Ingra answered, "Barrels."

Signe said, "Barrels and barrels and barrels."

I spoke my forming realization: "We can never allow Anthony de Marchand or his army to get those barrels."

The aliens on Lilly's ship had ammunition, boxes and crates of it. But they did not have barrels and barrels and barrels.

I thought about the destruction caused by the aliens, of the loss of Sven, the bullet I had taken in my chest and the ones that struck Torn — how they'd murdered the good Colonel Mathew Sparks as soon as he began to find the humanity hiding in his soul. I remembered the flashes of fire in the dark as they murdered each other and all the hurt and anger and pain that smeared the holiness of a ship on the medicine trail. I was silent a long time in my thoughts.

Freja said, "Poor man, I appreciate you must be exhausted after last night —" at which my mother blushed and Asa and Signe giggled. "But there are things that need to be done. We need to prepare."

"What has been done?" I directed my question to Asa.

"The scouts returned three days ago — just a half day before your own return. Every Summer Chief in the five valleys knows. Every Winter Chief is this morning being told. Every barrel of Dragon Blood we have has been hidden, with only one cask in each valley available for when we need it. If you are going to send out scouts to watch Anthony de Marchand's progress, we offer to send women with them."

Asa turned to look at Freja, and Freja nodded. She would go back out as a scout.

I saw the advantage. She would already know the where and the number.

I answered: "I will send out scouts immediately. The women can tell them everything they need to know before they go."

Signe said, "Hmm, you wish to protect us?"

I nodded.

She continued, "That was not what was put upon you this morning. What was put upon you was that you must consider the children and the women first in all your decisions. That does not mean we are to be held back. Yes, the men are warriors. You practise with your blades and your bows. You believe the warrior is in your spirit, that your grandfather's skill is in your muscle and your bone. But I ask you, Juha son of Torrey, how many murders occurred during this past Night of Anarchy?"

I answered, "None."

"True," she replied. The old woman sat with her hands clasped in her lap. "And it has been forty-seven years — ninety-four Nights of Anarchy — since there has been any violence in any of the five valleys. We are a peaceful people. The last army to march against the five valleys was led by the warlord James Helmetman, and that was two years before you were born. He did not make it even as far as the confluence. We confused him, and he and his army marched in circles on the stony plain until they were exhausted and went home."

Signe looked straight into my eyes. "My advice to you is be careful: your warriors have heart — they have confidence — but not one of them has ever been in a battle. Freja is as good a warrior as any of your men. Do not be afraid to seek her out."

Signe lowered her eyes in thought, then she said: "When Freja and the other scouts brought back the news, we women sat in a circle and looked forward. What is coming will be hard. In days to come, grief will fill the five valleys. People we love today will not be with us tomorrow. We did not see the end of the Björkan. But neither did we see us again in peace in the five valleys."

Signe spoke slowly, "You coupled last night with Freja. But you did not give her your child."

I looked toward Freja — tried to read her face but couldn't.

Signe continued, "Not for lack of trying. Freja knows she cannot be with child now and stopped it. She knows she will be needed for what is to come and cannot be with child. You know that a woman can couple with a man at any time of the year and conceive. And in years gone by, we did and babies were born. And the five valleys were populated. Both women and men like to copulate, and soon there were too many. Times became hard. The valley provides and it provides well. We have all we need. But if there are too many of us, we and the valley will suffer. So it came that copulation and baby-making only happen during the Night of Anarchy. And even then we must be careful. Not every woman able to bear children can be left to carry a seed."

Signe's voice shifted. Her tone had been that of the teacher. Now she spoke with authority:

"The number of the people in
the five valleys of the Björkan
shall equal the number of
the björka trees
standing alive in
those five valleys."

I had not known that. I had known generally but not precisely. I nodded.

My mother took her turn to speak. "It's a rare thing for the women to interfere in the selection of the Winter Chief."

I looked again at Freja. This time she smiled — a little mischief at the corners of her mouth.

Ingra continued, "We did not go against the men. Let's just say we augmented their decision. We chose you because you would understand. What you do or don't do will go far beyond your tenure as Winter Chief. In two hundred and five days, you will lay down your staff. Many of us will no longer be here.

"The future of the people of the five valleys is not in your strategies, in your intelligence, nor in your will. It is not in the strong hearts of the warriors.

"The future of the people
     of the five valleys is
          in our children.
"With everything you have,
     my son,
          with every bit of skill and
               knowledge that you possess,
                    with your mind,
                         your heart,
                              your body, and
                                   your soul,
                                        you must make sure,
                         when all is done,
                              the children will be
                                   able to grow up
                                        to replace those
                                             we lose."

When the women left, I went first to the abode of Torn, grabbed him by his ankles and dragged him from his bed. When I had him outside — when he was standing, his bare feet in the soil, his bare chest in the morning air — I told him what the women had told me. "It's not over, Torn. It's only just begun."

He put his hand upon my shoulder and asked, "What is it you need?"

I replied, "I need for you to accept the appointment of leader of the warriors."

Torn answered, "If the men will follow, I will lead."

"Then gather them — none are too young and none are too old. Organize them and arm them."

Torn asked, "Brother, can you still hear me in your mind when I send you my thoughts?"

I answered — my mind to his mind. "I can and I do. It seems the gift from Lilly did not end when we left her ship."

Torn the strategist replied, "We will teach this to our scouts before we send them out. We will know immediately what they see and hear."

. . .

The first report came on the third day of my tenure from the mind of the youth Magnus. "Anthony de Marchand builds a road across the stony plain."

Then he has not come to raid. He has come to stay. He won't be satisfied with a few barrels of Dragon Blood. I put myself in his place. What does an up-and-coming warlord need?

Warriors, of course, but he will have those he purchased — his apprentices. With guns he can raid and pillage and afford more. But others will flock to him when word spreads that he has weapons and he marches toward riches.

What else does a new warlord need beyond weapons and an army?

A fortress.

And there is no greater fortress in all the kingdoms and freeholds and unorganized lands on this planet than the five valleys of the Björkan. Anthony de Marchand wants everything we have — everything we love. He wants our home and our valleys.

There can be no retreat; there can be no surrender. If the Björkan are evicted from the five valleys, we will not survive. Cast into the open world, we will wither and die.

Five thinkers to advise me.

I chose Hildor,
> the oldest male in the fifth valley.

I chose Ragnar,
> the man who studied the river.

I chose Sievert,
> the man who understood ice.

I chose Torrey,
> my father and the previous Winter Chief, for his experience.

And I chose Signe,

the oldest woman not only in the fifth valley — Signe was the oldest person alive in all the five valleys.

We gathered in my new abode, sat each of us upon the floor. I might be Winter Chief, but among the thinkers, we are all of one mind.

Hildor spoke first: "Telling stories to hide the trail will not work this time. Anthony de Marchand will not become confused and wander the stony plain. He builds his own road. As he builds it, he creates a new and powerful story — a story shared by all who work on the construction of the road. They do not know they are putting together a story with each stone they place. They think all they are doing is making a road for carts and beasts and men."

I said, "No invader in the history of the five valleys has ever made it beyond the confluence. The warriors from the five valleys have always stopped them there. But not this time. The land around the confluence is open and flat — a place for battles between equally equipped armies. When we fought with bows and blades and lances against an army bruised and sore from crossing the stony plain, we expected a victory. We had fortified posts to withdraw to and regroup. We knew the land. We defended our homes. We had the psychological advantage. We have never been defeated.

But this time we will have no advantage. They will. They will come with the confidence of their new weapons, and when our men see one of their own killed by a bullet fired from a distance beyond the reach of a bow and see that bullet pierce armour, they will lose heart. If we go out to meet them — if we meet force with force — our men will be slaughtered."

Sievert said, "In that case, the first battle will by necessity be in the chasm. I think I can prepare a surprise for them. It will slow them down, but it won't stop them."

Signe said, "If you cannot stop them before they reach the chasm, you must stop them there. If you lose the chasm, you lose the valley."

The chasm we all knew — there was no reason to speak of it — was a hundred and fifty tree lengths long, sheer ice walls on both sides rising a hundred tree lengths straight up. Down its centre ran the river. From late summer until the beginning of the spring melt, when the river is at its lowest, there is room on each side between the river and the ice. It was never wider than a single tree length. In many places, the river runs so close to the ice that men must pass in single file.

Our ability to walk on water will be no advantage. Standing on the river, we would be exposed to their guns, and no one — no matter how skilled in walking on water — can concentrate enough to stay on the surface and engage in a battle at the same time.

Ragnar spoke, "We have a chance — it's a long chance — but maybe if we dam the river above the chasm and hold back the water until Anthony de Marchand and all his men are in the chasm, then release the water, we could flush them out."

Torrey said, "That would be a major undertaking. The river will not be easily held back. If you want to build a dam, you must start now and you must engage every person in the valley in its construction."

He turned to Signe, "How many bolts of björka silk are stored away?"

She answered, "Hundreds."

I asked, "Can we get them sewn into bags? We will fill the bags with earth to build the dam."

Ragnar said, "We will need more than sandbags to hold our river. We will need to move boulders for braces — at least one large boulder every tree length."

Later, when I told Torn, he replied, "That was what I was looking for — some place for the men to hide behind. We can fight guns with bows. But we need to be sheltered and they must be within range."

THE MEETING

The Winter Chiefs of the five valleys agreed to meet at the confluence. Four of us sat in a circle beside the rush of the river as we waited for the fifth. Dalmar of the first valley could be seen in the distance walking with a dozen of his people.

I looked southward across the stony plain. I did not see Anthony de Marchand or his army.

Freja stood behind me. I asked, "How far?"

She replied, "Still five days at steady."

I calculated aloud. "It takes seven days at a steady march to cross the stony plain. Marchand has been building his road for twenty days. So if he continues at this rate, he will be here in another fifty days."

Junis of the third valley said, "We have time then."

Bosse of the second valley said, "He won't make it

here. We will stop him and bury him among the stones of the plain."

I said no more until Dalmar arrived and found his place in the circle, his people standing behind him.

He was of the first valley, so he spoke first: "The last time the Chiefs of the five valleys gathered here at the confluence, we celebrated at the summer solstice, the five hundred years of the Björkan occupancy of the five valleys. I am told it was a party greater than any Night of Anarchy. We feasted and sang and danced and copulated for five days and five nights. And the next year, forty-seven babies were born in the same week. None of us here were alive then. So this has fallen to us. This is the test of our generation. In times past when an enemy approached, each valley sent their warriors to the confluence, and the warriors chose their leader from among their number and made their plans and strategies. Never in the history of the five valleys has an enemy ever progressed beyond this confluence."

At this Dalmar stood, took up his staff with the head of an ice fox carved as his crest, and drove it firmly into the ground. "Anthony de Marchand — the bastard from Öland — shall not win beyond here. I make my oath on behalf of the people of the first valley."

Bosse of the second valley spoke quieter than Dalmar. He spoke of his love for the children. He offered to personally lead his warriors onto the stony plain to meet the enemy. A winter hawk crested the staff he drove into the ground with his pledge to never surrender the confluence.

Junis of the third valley rose and looked out across the stony plain. His face appeared troubled; his voice rasped as he spoke: "I am concerned. The third valley has a wealth of women and a dearth of warriors. We cannot afford to lose even a few. If I pledge my warriors to defend the confluence and it goes badly, I will not have warriors left to protect the third valley. Here is my staff." He held it up for us to see. "The drops carved along its length are for the rain that waters the björka tree — the rain that comes in the spring and turns our valleys green. I will pledge my staff to defend all the people of the five valleys as much as I am able. But my first pledge — the pledge put upon me twelve days ago — was to protect the third valley and to remember the children and the women first in all my decisions. This was not a pledge that I made; this was not a pledge of my choosing. It was put upon me and because it was put upon me by the people of the third valley — the people who gave me life, who stood me on my feet and nurtured me and kept me — I cannot breach it."

Dalmar and Bosse squirmed. It was obvious they wished to answer. But it was not their turn to speak. The turn belonged to Ola of the fourth valley.

"Winter Chiefs."

He nodded to

each of us in turn.

We nodded in return.

"This is a beautiful day. The sun still has warmth. My blood flows in my body and it, too, has warmth. My heart is warm and my mind is at peace. The people of the fourth valley have enough food to make it through the coming winter. We have all that we need and we have an excess that we can share. We wish for nothing belonging to or claimed by another. One hundred and seven warriors reside in the fourth valley. For decades and decades, we have shaped our weapons and our armour. We have practised our skills and studied the art of war.

"We have also studied music and mathematics. We have studied the water and the ice and the things that grow upon the ground and the things that grow beneath the ground. We have studied the animals that fly, the animals that walk, the animals that crawl, those that swim and those that slither.

"We have studied the stars and we have studied what it means to be brothers. Among my one hundred and seven warriors are eleven women. The women of the fourth valley put life into our valley, and they have assured me that they will defend that life with their lives. We men can do no less."

I spoke next. "I am Juha Torrey's son of the fifth valley. I have recently returned from a journey among the stars and have some information for the people of the five valleys. The man who marches against us betrayed Torn, Sven, and me to the aliens in exchange for firearms.

"Nothing in our history — nothing known — has ever been found to be stronger than properly dried björka wood." I looked to Ola of the fourth valley. "Your people have made a study of the björka. You know that when the cells of the björka dry out, they collapse inward on themselves, and that is the source of the björka's strength. You know the reason that arrows made from heartwood are straight is because the fibres of the björka are straightest there. You have made a study of the curves that give our bows their force and their range."

I turned again to the gathered Chiefs and their councils. "We have over the centuries made our armour thinner and thinner, taking pride in its lightness. Our armour will stop blades and arrows — even a lance. But I assure you, our armour does not stop bullets. Anthony de Marchand and his army will be here in fifty days. Björka wood takes a full year to dry. We do not have time to make thicker armour — even if we knew how thick was thick enough.

"Old strategies will not win against new weapons. It is true: no enemy has ever won beyond this confluence. It is true: our warriors fight out of love for the valleys and love for the people of the valleys. And love has always won over anger and greed. But bullets can pierce our armour and our shields. Bullets can kill even a heart that is filled with love.

"Brothers, we need new strategies. Anthony de Marchand is just a man. But he has studied and planned. We must not underestimate his cunning — it is driven by his cravings. He has dreamt of being a warlord all his days and will not make rash mistakes. He does not come to raid. He comes to take. He does not want our armour and our blades. He wants the five valleys. He wants this ice fortress. He wants your homes."

  I waited for what I had said to settle,
      waited while the other four Chiefs
         brought their minds to this new place
           with all its implications.

Freja spoke. "Chiefs," she said. "Thinkers." She bent a knee formally. "Juha's guess is probably right. Anthony de Marchand wants our five valleys because they are natural fortresses. The five valleys are arranged like the five leaves of the medicine plant — each leaf has a stem that joins it to the others. The stems to our valleys are the five chasms that meet here at the confluence. It is these stems that hold us together — so it is these stems, the chasms, that we must defend."

Dalmar answered, "Sister, you are right. We are joined by the stems and those stems are defendable. The chasms are a formidable defence. But if we each go to our own valley, then each valley must stand alone and defend its chasm from within. We will be divided."

Torn strode to the centre of the circle and turned as he spoke directly to one Chief and then another. "If we brought out every warrior from every valley, we would have about three hundred men and maybe forty women. If we brought out every man who lives like a woman, we would have another dozen. If we brought out every youth — male or female — able to hold a blade or a bow, we could count another twenty. That might seem like a mighty force, but a forty-five-calibre Browning holds seven bullets. A rifle holds thirty bullets that come out the end of the barrel as fast as the trigger is pressed. If Anthony de Marchand comes with a mere dozen rifles, he can kill every man, woman, and child that stands at the confluence in about ten heartbeats. We can stand together. But if we do, we will die together."

THE ONSLAUGHT

We shared strategies of dams to hold back water to flush the chasms, and of barricades for our warriors to stand behind.

Ragnar the thinker, who studied the river, met with the river experts from the other valleys.

Sievert met with the experts who studied ice.

We taught the scouts how to send messages with their minds.

And we counted our arrows. We did not have time to shape more, and the number we had we knew were too few.

After we shared our knowledge, we each went back to our valleys to prepare and to wait.

We built our dam — our barricade of boulders and sandbags — across the river. We closed in our valley from ice wall to ice wall. Luck was not with us. The weather turned cool. The ice melt that fed the river slowed, and the water behind our dam rose only slowly. Ragnar was constant: checking the dam, measuring the water rise, walking the length of the valley, talking to the river — begging.

Torn trained the warriors. We had seventy-seven. Eight of them were women. We counted eleven youths big enough to draw a bow. In the fifth valley, there were four men who preferred to live like women. Three of them chose to stay with the bulk of the women — the fourth said he still felt like a woman but had muscle enough to draw a bow and would stand with the warriors at the barricade.

First light brightened the sky above the fifth valley. I heard the youth Magnus in my mind: "Hey Juha, look at this."

I closed my eyes to better see the image he was sending me. Anthony de Marchand's army was at the confluence; his camp had carts and cart beasts. I estimated a quick count of his men — clearly over a hundred, probably closer to two.

I whispered a thought to Magnus. "Can you get around them to make your way back to the valley? Once they are in the chasm, you will be blocked."

He answered, "I could if I wished, but I will stay out here and be your eyes and ears."

The image he sent turned downward until I could

see he was wearing a button coat with plenty of buttons remaining and a heavy hem.

I sent him a soft, "Be careful and stay out of sight."

He answered, "I will."

Ice surrounds the confluence on three sides, surrounds Anthony de Marchand, his army and his camp. Sievert knows ice, has made a study of it — understands its essence and its substance. He is not alone; many in the five valleys understand ice.

But it seems Anthony de Marchand — in all his visits — didn't pay attention. He made his camp in the perfect auditorium.

Our musicians — one from each valley — climbed to the top of the ice with nyckelharpor and hollow tubes upon their backs. When they drew their bows across the strings, fingers easy upon the keys, their music flowed out of each nyckelharpa down the hollow tubes into the ice.

Sievert explained to me, "Ice is made of crystals. Each crystal the music passes through clarifies the sound before it travels to the next. What Anthony de Marchand and his army are hearing is music purified thousands upon thousands of times."

We in the five valleys could also hear the music, just as clearly as our visitors at the confluence. Nyckelharpa music is sweet sounds made sweeter — given breadth and depth and tune and tone and volume through the ice.

We call our masters of music Spelmen. For that is exactly what they do. Through the instruments they play — through the music they make — they cast spells. And what a spell they played.

Every warrior standing
at our barricade
laid down their bow,
ignored their blade,
turned their eyes to
the sky and
cried.
Cried for the dead lost
in all the wars.
Cried for the hurt caused
by men.
Cried for those that lived and
suffered.

The tune changed — another Spelman played and our eyes fell to the earth and we cried again, shed tears of joy filled with pure euphoria, knowing that this minute we are alive, this minute we are loved. The music filled us and we were full — so full — our hearts ached to contain it all.

Sievert was still standing beside me. I said to him, "I need to see Anthony de Marchand's camp. But I don't seem able to rouse our scout at the moment. He must be caught by the music too."

Sievert replied, "Let me show you," then led the way to the ice wall. There he wiped a patch with the palm of his hand, breathed on the patch and polished it a bit more. He put his forehead on the ice, cupped his hands to the sides of his head to block the light, and looked into the polished patch. Then he stepped back and, with a wave of his hand, offered the view to me.

When I looked through the polished ice, I saw the confluence in panorama. I saw Anthony de Marchand's camp. I saw his men sitting on the ground, their weapons cast aside. Even his cart beasts had lain down.

The music played
      night and day,
            day and night.

Spelmen took turns. They took long rests between their solos, then put their hands and arms — their hearts and minds, their souls — into their music.

Everyone who heard — who listened — learned to love their own breath with easy in and out, to love their own heartbeat as it kept time, kept life.

We went about our daily tasks, all thoughts of war taken and driven out. Men could be seen laughing or crying, dancing or humming. Wherever the music took them, they went with love. Love for themselves — filled to full and overflowed.

Love for all,
      all who walked,

all who swam,
all who flew,
all who slithered and
all and
all and
all.

. . .

It was Anthony de Marchand himself who broke the spell. I watched the transformation through the eyes of the young scout Magnus, watched Anthony de Marchand fight with himself — twisting and struggling — as he tore at his clothes and pulled at his hair.

And I wondered, *Why can this man not love himself? What has he done that he cannot forgive himself?*

Then I watched as he went from one of his soldiers to the next and plugged their ears, shouted orders, dragged men to their feet, and shoved rifles back into their hands. It seemed love could be defeated with hate.

Anthony de Marchand chose to attack the fifth valley first — the same morning as he stopped the ears of his men.

Magnus shouted in my mind: "He's coming!"

I didn't need to tell Torn; he'd heard. "Don't worry, Juha," he said as he rushed toward the chasm. "We have arranged a surprise for Marchand."

Not long after, we heard gunshots coming from deep within the chasm. The warriors on the barricade were prepared. But Anthony de Marchand's men did not come.

Later that afternoon, Torn explained, "Sievert showed us how to put our reflections into the ice. So we were both within and without at the same time. Where the river forced his men to walk close to the ice wall, we were waiting — standing just inside the ice — and thrust outward with our lances into their sides. They fired at our reflections, wasted bullets as they retreated. They will be slow coming back."

But they weren't. Marchand's army rushed up the chasm again. This time with shields at their sides when they came close to the ice wall. We saw them coming. Ragnar tripped the release at the centre of the dam and the river flooded into the chasm to meet them — to greet them. We welcomed them with water. They were flushed out — soaked and made to swim — but none were drowned.

Ragnar's plan needed the river to fill behind our dam, and the river had not joined in the plan — or rather, the cooler than normal weather reduced the melt and left the river weakened.

The next morning after the waters had subsided, Anthony de Marchand sent his men again into the chasm. This time they came within arrow range of the barricade. Our archers held them back. We learned something in this first exchange. Either their firearms were not accurate or their warriors had not practised enough. Bullets thudded into the sandbags or whizzed overhead, but none of our warriors were hit.

Hildor kept score. In the first exchange, we wounded four in the chasm when our reflections ambushed them — one of those possibly mortally. Our arrows found seven when they came within range of the barricade — five were clearly killed. They fired forty-six rounds at the ice during the ambush and another hundred and fourteen or maybe fifteen during the first exchange. They were firing too fast for Hildor to count with precision. He apologized.

We gave up nine arrows.

Our youth either needed more practice or needed to be instructed not to loose an arrow until and unless they knew it would mean a kill.

I asked, "How many arrows do we have left?"

Hildor answered, "Four hundred and thirty-seven."

"How many lances?"

"One for each warrior and a dozen spare."

I saw through Magnus's eyes the piling of stones — five mounds the first day and another two the day after. Out of the hundred and eighty-two who first marched against us, one hundred and seventy-five remained alive. Two of those lay on their pallets wounded.

After that Anthony de Marchand kept his men in their camp.

We could not leave our valley — but then, we did not want to. It was a standoff.

THE CAPTIVE

While we waited, we added to the barricade — filled in again the gap in the dam to hold back the river. But Ragnar did not have much hope. That time of year, the river flowed too slowly.

Åke taught the youth archership — how to breathe into the release and set an arrow free. But not free to wander in its flight.

He taught them to
 follow the arrow with
  their mind,
   how to steer and to
    guide an arrow to
    its target.

Just before daybreak on the twenty-third day after the first attack, I awoke to the sound of Magnus screaming: "Torn! Juha! I'm caught!"

In his panic, Magnus was not sending images, only his voice filled with fear.

I heard Torn tell him, "Easy, Magnus, easy. Take a breath and show us."

The images that came from his terrified mind were a jumble of stones and boots.

I told Torn, "He's being dragged along the ground."

Torn responded, "Look up, Magnus, look up. Let us see where you are. Easy now, easy, you've got this. Your mind is in control. Your heart still beats, your lungs still breathe. This minute you are alive, and because you are alive you are in control. Now show me where you are so I can come get you."

Magnus did not need to look up. He was at that moment jerked to his feet. Anthony de Marchand stood in front of him. I heard his words to Magnus: "What do we have here? A filthy little spy. Do you know what we do to spies?"

I saw the fist coming. Anthony de Marchand punched young Magnus in the face. I felt the pain in my cheekbone. I tasted blood. Then the images and voices stopped, as Magnus must have lost mind control.

Anthony de Marchand was quick to send a messenger. The man must have run.

I stood at the barricade, Torn and Freja beside me. The man spoke: "I am unarmed. I bring only a message. Anthony de Marchand, the Lord of the North, sends you an offer. He will trade — in equal measure — Dragon Blood for all the blood in the boy. Blood for blood. You have until the sun touches the horizon to deliver one keg of Dragon Blood. If you delay beyond that time, Anthony de Marchand, the Lord of the North, says you can bring a lesser measure tomorrow because he will begin draining the blood from the boy. One bowlful every time the sun goes down until the boy is dry."

I sat with the thinkers. Torn and Freja sat with us.

I told them, "Here is what we know. Anthony de Marchand has ambitions over all the north. He has styled himself a lord. And he is short on Dragon Blood. He has told us that which he needs the most."

Hildor spoke the obvious because it needed saying. "If you give him a keg of Dragon Blood, he will use it to kill many more than Magnus."

Signe spoke the other truth:
"The life of Magnus is
    worth the lives of
        every one of us.
"No life is worth more or
    less than any
        other life or
            any number of
                lives.

"His life is worth mine and
 yours and
  every one of us.
"Your choice, Juha, is
 not a mathematical calculation.
  You cannot choose based upon
   one choice having more
    worth than
     the other choice."

Torn said, "I promised Magnus I would come get him. He is waiting for me."

Freja said, "And I am coming with you."

Hildor touched Signe's hand. She turned toward him and the two old people looked into each other's eyes. Then Hildor spoke. "A rush attack on their camp might free the boy, but it also might make our situation worse. Better to go slow. Sievert and Ragnar, we need you to work together — to bring ice and water together."

The two thinkers looked at each other and grinned — of course, when water and ice combine they make fog.

Hildor continued, "Signe and I have a few more ways to hide you and a few more surprises that Anthony de Marchand might not expect."

In our preparations, I reached out to Magnus. "Young warrior, can you show me or tell me how you are bound?"

He replied, "I am bound with jute rope — hand and foot — to a stake in the centre of their camp."

I told him, "We are coming to get you. Be patient."

When I told Signe, she said, "Jute rope — that's easy. If Freja is part of the rescue, I will tell her what she must do."

Torn chose three warriors to accompany him:
Enar,
    Freja,
        and Gunne.

Before they left, Hildor told a silent story to their shoes. They walked away not making a sound.

Ragnar and Sievert met them at the beginning of the chasm and spoke to the river and the ice. The cascading water hushed and all seemed still before it began to hiss quietly.

The four rescuers took the lizard Signe had caught for them, walked into the ensuing fog an hour before sunset, and disappeared from sight.

Later Freja told me how it went. "At first walking was difficult. There were four of us trying to see out of that little lizard's eyes. It was not bad if you walked right behind it — then you could see where to put your feet. But if you walked to one side, you had to be more careful. Using a lizard's eyes takes about the same amount of concentration as walking on water — you really must stay focused.

"Sievert and Ragnar must have talked to the other valleys. When we got to the confluence, fog poured out of all five chasms. Torn could hear Magnus in the centre of Anthony de Marchand's camp, but the lizard could not see far enough for us to find him.

"I told a story to the jute rope that bound Magnus, told it to slither away and bind another. Then Magnus was able to come toward us as we went toward him.

"We bumped into men — or they bumped into us. Because they couldn't see, they couldn't tell if we were friend or foe. We could have slain a dozen easily, but Torn would not allow it. 'We do not kill like that,' he said."

I asked, "And Magnus — is he alright?"

Freja answered, "Yes, Magnus is fine. We got him before he was harmed. The fog was so thick. No one would have been able to tell when sunset occurred or even if it occurred at all. None of his blood was shed."

I asked, "Where is he?"

Freja told me, "He's with the women. They're taking care of him. He is fine in body and limb. But tonight they will doctor his mind."

I didn't see Magnus until nearly zenith the next day. The first thing he said was, "Chief Juha, what is a canon?"

I answered, "An ancient law, one that is written — something that cannot be easily changed. Why do you ask?"

He said, "That's what I thought too. But I heard Anthony de Marchand's men say they were going to get a cannon to take out our barricade."

They stormed the chasm. Anthony de Marchand committed his entire force to the attack. They came pushing behind the iron barrel on wheels. When they won to the inner end of the chasm, they fired their cannon at our barricade. The echoes from the explosion brought down great chunks from the ice walls. Some of his men were crushed.

The shot tore into our barricade,
tore through the sandbags,
tore through the body of Jon.
Jon died with his eyes open,
his mouth open, and
his body torn open.

Anthony de Marchand's men fired their cannon again. Again ice fell from the walls. Again some of his men were injured. Again the shell hit our barricade — tore through it, tore through another warrior. Björn was hit in the hip. He lived to be dragged back to the women.

When a large part of a body is ripped away, doctoring cannot put it back again.

Björn struggled to live, and the women struggled to keep him alive.

It became clear very quickly that we could not hold

the barricade — that sandbags would not protect our warriors. Two more were broken when Marchand's army fired the cannon for the third time.

The brothers Erik and Lars stood together during life and lay together in death. That night their mother would wail until her throat was raw and her voice croaked.

We could not tell stories to put our men back together again — their wounds were too great; they were too broken. Their injuries went beyond our imaginations. We were left without sufficient words. And besides, no man could concentrate enough to tell a mending story while cannon fire smashed the barricade and rifle fire kept our warriors' heads down.

They didn't need Torn to tell them to withdraw. Our warriors broke and ran.

Ragnar had presence of mind enough to trip the dam, and the river flowed into the chasm. But there was not enough water to flush them out — only enough to hold them back while we retreated to the trees.

When the sun dazzled the valley with its setting, Anthony de Marchand owned the barricade and the southern tip of the fifth valley. The invaders occupied our valley; they were in our home. Our hearts were broken. The women and the children wept as they gathered a few necessary items before they fled to the far north end of

the fifth valley of the Björkan,
the fifth valley of the Björkan,
the fifth valley of the Björkan.
Not so —
not anymore.
It was still the fifth valley,
but it did not belong
to the Björkan
alone.

Our warriors took shelter where they could find it — behind boulders or preferably behind a björka tree. Something familiar, something friendly, something they believed would protect them.

I was not the only one that night who felt their heart break — who cried.

Somehow Hildor found me in the deepest part of the dark. He reported, "Björn told the women he did not want to stay here anymore. The women let him go. They put him under a björka and he breathed his last breath. We have four dead:

"Björn,
Jon,
Erik, and
Lars.

"I am certain seven of our warriors are wounded. They cannot hide their injuries — gashes to their faces or blood-soaked clothing. I suspect another five because they limp or favour one side over the other, but they deny they are hurt.

"I am only certain we killed two of Anthony de Marchand's men. I am sorry but I, too, was keeping my head down during their attack and did not watch it all. How many arrows do you have?"

I counted, then answered, "Five."

Hildor said, "You have more than most. We gave up far too many. Our men were firing wild. With the arrows in your quiver, we have three hundred and twenty-six left."

That would be enough if we were of sound mind and had strong hearts. There was more than one arrow for every one of Anthony de Marchand's men.

It was my job to ease the warriors' minds and strengthen their hearts. I planned to slip around to each as soon as it became light. To bring them cheer and share resolve — to remind them of the women and the children.

I never got the chance. Before sunrise — when it was barely light — Anthony de Marchand's men began chopping down björka trees. The sound of an iron axe into the soft flesh of a living tree was horror enough to cause any Björkan to weep.

Heartache upon
    heartache.
        How much more
            could we take?

I heard Torn's voice shouting.

"Enough.

    Get up.

        If you hide behind a björka tree,

            you will die behind a björka tree.

            On your feet.

"If we are going to die

    we will die defending,

        not hiding.

"Get in front of the trees — they need you to protect them.

"Up.

    Up.

        If you are going to die,

            die fighting."

This was Torn the warrior — the warrior I first saw in action on Lilly's spaceship.

THREE

THE RETURN

I heard Juha. Heard him in his hour of grief — when he released his pain to the universe. I spoke to my sisters. They agreed we should go. We should go because good people should not have to stand alone.

Seven of us aboard our little ship:

Mari,

Hillevi,

Irja,

Sora,

Dakini,

Ulla, and

myself as Ship Mother.

Sora, whose name means sky, and Dakini, whose name means walks in the sky, were known on our world as the women who could propel a ship the fastest.

Hillevi the woman of war and Mari the rebellious came along for the action. I was glad to see Irja the woman of peace — she would be needed.

Ulla the powerful balanced the crew. She had within her the power of peace and the power of war.

Our ship was small and fast — less than half the size of the medicine-gathering ship where I first met Juha and his brother Torn. With seven of us pushing we would not take long, but the distance was great and we might not be there as soon as Juha needed.

I reached out to him, sent my mind across the gap between Andromeda and the Milky Way.

I don't think he heard me.

I sent anyway —

sent that someone cared about him,

sent that he was needed,

sent that he was strong,

sent that he was loved.

When I listened I did not hear him reply. I spoke across the distance to Torn. He heard me. He had been lying down, his ear to the ground. I reached out to Hillevi and Mari. Those warrior women sent their thoughts to Torn. We sensed him when he leapt to his feet and began shouting.

Then I called to all my sisters and we sent across the reach to all the people in the five valleys of the Björkan. One strong message: "Hold on."

As fast as we could propel our ship, we set out. Concentration. Focus the mind. Create a tunnel from here to the fifth valley. Pour the mind into it. Seek Juha's world.

The thought tunnel created by the seven of us to propel our little ship grew. I could see out the other end. I could see the invaders hacking down björka trees. I cringed.

"Careful," I spoke aloud. "Careful now. Do not upset the balance."

They couldn't hear — or they didn't listen. Another björka fell, and another.

Hillevi asked, "Don't they know what will happen?"

I answered, "No one told them."

She said, "If they free the dragons, we're going to need help."

That was true. Not even the best Björkan storyteller could tell a dragon back into a tree. Mari and Hillevi were warrior-like, but even they could not fight dragons. We were firstly medicine women. We were healers; we made things better.

We pushed harder — hurried our little vessel, drove our minds forward.

Thought is fast — faster than light, faster than the force of the universe — but even with seven pushing with all our minds, we could see we would be too late.

Irja suggested, "Maybe we should stop first at Hamra to ask the Valkyries to ride with us."

Sora joked, "Maybe it would be better to invite the dragons."

I asked, "Have any of you been to a dragon planet before?"

All shook their heads and Sora let her smile wane.

I had been to Dra-kai. Once.

Dragon skin is medicine — we had travelled there to gather what they shed. Even though the dragons had not seen us, it was pure terror to walk among them.

Their worlds inspire
> the ideas of Hades,
>> of hell,
>>> of damnation,
>>>> of torment and
>>>>> forever and ever.

It's not that dragons are immortal; they are not. But they do live a very long time — longer than the civilizations that experience them. Their long lives seem forever to any other.

I was Ship Mother. It would be my decision. Did we stop at Hamra to invite the Valkyries to ride with us or stay the course? The delay would only be a matter of days — a matter of asking and then a matter of living with the consequences.

I looked through the long tunnel to the five valleys.

If we got there in time, we could walk invisible among the invaders, snatch their guns from their hands. If we got there in time.

I heard myself sigh. Why couldn't we — all of us on all the planets where dragons were subdued — put our minds together, pool our knowledge, share our understanding?

Instead of this,

    this that happens

        when it need not happen.

On every planet where tetrapodal beings evolved to rule, their greatest danger has always been themselves. We are the cause of our own suffering. There is no animal more dangerous to a human than a human — except, of course, dragons.

I heard Irja in my thoughts, "I've made contact."

I asked, "With whom?"

She answered, "Signe, an Elder from the fifth valley. She will let the others know we are coming."

I asked, "What does she know about the fallen björka?"

Irja answered, "Signe was remembering a story when my thoughts reached her — a story about how the dragons were put into the trees. Like every planet that received life spores, hers also had two kinds: four-limbed earth-walkers and dragons. And like on every planet with life, they warred. Only there they did not destroy one another; they made a truce. The people did not eradicate the dragons, and the dragons did not eradicate the people. The dragons could continue to live but would live inside the björka trees. There they would be nourished and kept."

I had heard this story before, but it was good to be reminded. There had been a truce — a Human–Dragon Treaty. Now the people were breaking their promise. The dragons would not differentiate between the people of the valleys and the invaders. A dragon sleeping in a björka tree — awoken by an axe — would think itself betrayed and in danger. It would not negotiate even if there were any who remembered its language.

War would be its only waking thought.

THE VALKYRIES

I reached out to our sisters on the planet Hamra. Why they named it after a hammer I do not know; Valkyries prefer swords.

They agreed — eagerly.

We didn't have to go far out of our way to get them. Their desire for a fight, and maybe their wings, allowed them to jump to our ship while we were still a day away.

Once we had them on board,
    all twenty-four,
        our placid ship
           was not peaceful
            anymore.

It seems a Valkyrie cannot speak without screaming. And of course they brought their horses — horses that screamed louder than their riders. Horses that ate the foliage of the little ship's plants.

Rota led them. But I doubt by command — no one could command this horde. She led simply by going first.

Not only did we not lose time in stopping to pick up the Valkyries, they helped to push our ship faster. Rota screamed, "To the front! To the front! Come, sisters! We need to sail this vessel — all hands on deck!" Then she grabbed the mane of her horse, leapt onto its back, and led a charge toward the leading edge of our vessel.

Twenty-four winged Valkyries on charging horses, all in a line at the front of our ship — screaming with all their might, their horses galloping.

And seven medicine women in quiet concentration. We more than tripled our speed.

A day and

    a day and

        we would be there.

I called out to Juha, "Hold on!"

I heard his reply, "It is too late, Lilly. It is too late."

I yelled a thought at him, "It is not too late — you still breathe.

"Keep breathing.

    Keep breathing, Juha.

        Help comes."

He answered, his thought strong, "They came looking for the blood of the dragon — now the dragons want their blood."

I asked, "And the people of the fifth valley?"

Juha answered, "Huddled together at the northern-most tip. Sievert and the ice experts from the other valleys work together to carve a passage. As of this morning, still only reflections can traverse the ice. They are working on re-forming the reflection when it gets to the next valley. When they master that story, we will send the children. But the dragons are hungry and won't stop after they have feasted on Anthony de Marchand's army. They will come for us."

I heard Rota's voice interrupt our conversation. "Any swallow tails?"

I asked Juha.

He answered, "Signe asked the same. Yes. There is at least one with a split tail."

Rota yelled, "Damn!"

Juha must have heard. He replied, "Signe said the same."

I comforted. "Hold on, Juha. By the time the sun rises over the five valleys of the Björkan tomorrow, help will be there."

Our ship would not be there, but we could send the Valkyries ahead. With seven medicine women helping with the transfer and the eagerness of the warriors to join the battle, we could send this horde and their horses ahead. We would be there a day later.

THE ENGAGEMENT

Twenty-four women with wings and swords riding war horses. Twenty-four women with wings — naked — who'd never known more clothing than a beaded choker and breastplate. With hair that had never known a brush.

No, they were not gods. But they could easily be mistaken for divinity. They defied rational rules; they defied gravity. Women riding winged horses makes sense. Winged women riding horses does not. Maybe it was their screaming that warped the laws of physics. More likely, it was the sheer force of their will.

I have been on the medicine trail for a very long time. I have been to most of the living planets in the seven galaxies. I have known many races of beings and cultures of peace and cultures of war and cultures that want only to be. I think I know bravery; I've seen it before. But to ride naked into a rage of dragons — without a shield or a speck of cloth … My imagination failed me.

I wished I was with Juha looking upward in the morning when a horde of Valkyries came screaming from the sky — swords flashing in the dawn, a thunder of hooves. Dream-heavy dragons awakened by the charge. To watch the battle between flame and steel — between flesh and scale. Heavily armoured dragons dressed in plate against the flesh of women.

A sky melee,
       a sky of fire and
              a sky of screams.

Twenty-four Valkyries sped from our ship that morning — greedily seeking the encounter, craving battle. It did not go well for them. The swallow tail dragon surprised them with her speed. Skuld was bathed in dragon breath when she played the decoy. She was chased from the sky, clawed and clutched as she fell. Then to add insult, the swallow tail did not eat her catch, but dropped her to a larger male.

Without Skuld to hold it up, her horse fell, smashed itself upon the ice.

The first battle went to the dragons.

· · ·

We arrived just before the next zenith. Seven medicine women began ministering to the people of the fifth valley. The men refused our help until they were assured the children and the women had been cared for. The children and the women needed only to be sheltered. They'd been driven from their abodes when they had become undefendable. Their circle in the centre of the fifth valley had been designed as a school, not a fortress. It offered no protection from invaders. They hid in the forest, clustered at the northernmost end of their valley — the men between them and the invading army.

I asked Rota, the lead Valkyrie, "Do you have a plan?"

She answered, "No."

Her horse stood behind her, its head over her shoulder. The sun was well into its descent; another hour maybe of daylight.

I asked, "Then what do you intend to do?"

She answered, "Kill dragons."

All the Valkyries screamed:

"KILL DRAGONS!

 KILL DRAGONS!

  KILL DRAGONS!"

They frenzied. Those on horseback rode in circles. Those afoot raised their swords and screeched a long, high-pitched war cry. When it began the hairs on the back of my neck stood up. As it increased the force of it made me step back, made my heart pound and my mind spin.

When their cry ended every voice in the fifth valley was silent — even the wind was hushed. Rota lowered her sword and held it across her chest. She said, "You cannot plan to kill dragons because dragons do not plan to be dragons."

She stepped closer — her horse followed — and lowered her voice a few octaves. "I have fought dragons on many planets — whenever we have been called to restore the balance. There are worlds where dragons rule. We do not go there. Those are their worlds. This is the only place in all the galaxies we know of where humans and dragons peacefully co-existed, and only because the dragons agreed to remain in the trees. But now the truce is broken and we are left with no choice. We either eradicate the dragons now, or they will turn this into a dragon world.

"The ancestors of these people must have been strong to bind the dragons. I do not see any here today with that kind of strength. So again, Valkyries ride to war — to glory.

"I know on many worlds we have visited in time gone by — they tell stories that we will come again on the last days to battle evil. Those are misconceptions. We do not come to battle evil and bring about the end of the world and carry the people away to heaven or feast hall in Valhalla. We promised we would return if we were needed to restore the balance on their planets."

Again a screech arose from the Valkyries:

"KILL DRAGONS!

KILL DRAGONS!

KILL DRAGONS!"

They mounted their horses and screamed into the sky.

THE MESSENGER

Snow began to fall in large, heavy globs that filled the sky.

I met with Juha, Signe, and Hildor. "We could transport the children and women to one of the other valleys," I offered.

Signe replied, "That would only overcrowd someone else's abode. It would do nothing about the dragons."

I asked, "How many are there?"

Juha answered, "Eleven. Three burst forth from trees in our valley; the other eight from trees in the other valleys."

Signe offered, "There may be more that have not yet awakened. We have no way of knowing." Snow covered her head and shoulders. She shivered.

Hillevi and Mari approached. They carried rifles.

Mari explained, "We walked among the invaders;

they are crammed in the chasm. We were able to snatch these from the first few, but when we tried to grab the weapon from Anthony de Marchand, he held on. Now he has ordered his men to hold on to theirs, and some have taken to tying their weapons to their wrists."

Juha said, "Of course, the dragons are eating them too. The safest place is in the chasms — the dragons will have trouble flying in there. But it's not a solution. When the dragons want, they will just walk into the chasms and feed. It's going to be a hard winter for everyone."

Signe said, "Then we can return to our abodes. We are not safe from the dragons there, but we are not safe from the dragons here either. With Anthony de Marchand cringing in the chasm, at least we won't have to worry about any of the children being shot."

Hildor fidgeted with his bone and bead choker and said, "Each dragon eats one person per day. And there are eleven dragons. In a hundred days there will not be a single person left in any of the five valleys — including Anthony de Marchand and his entire army. Then the dragons will go out in search of a new food source." He lowered his head and ran his hand through his grey hair. "In the eight days since the dragons broke free from their trees, seven of our warriors have been eaten. We were lucky. In the other valleys more were taken. Our scouts tell us Anthony de Marchand has been offering cart beasts to the dragons, hoping to keep them from eating his men. He is quickly running out of cart beasts."

Juha said, "Too bad dragon plate is bulletproof."

Hildor looked up. "He tried using his cannon. They missed. The swallow tail dragon grabbed it and flew away. It is somewhere out on the ice now."

Juha spoke plain truth: "Our only hope lies with the Valkyries."

A shout from the forest. "Messenger coming!"

One of Anthony de Marchand's men — Torn walked behind him, an arrow nocked in his bow.

The messenger stood with arms down and his palms facing us. "Anthony de Marchand, the Lord of the North, seeks a truce with the people of the fifth valley. He asks to join forces against the dragons."

Torn seethed. "Let Anthony de Marchand first renounce his claim to lordship of the north, then maybe we will join forces — but only maybe."

The messenger replied, "Anthony de Marchand, the Lord of the North, says he is prepared to negotiate with the people of the valleys. He says the dragons sleep in the early afternoon. He says there will be an hour when we will not have to watch the skies."

I laughed. I shouldn't have but it just came out. "The Valkyries are not going to let the dragons sleep in the afternoon."

Signe spoke mind-to-mind, mostly to Juha, but we all heard. "He might be able to help."

Juha replied to the messenger. "Tell Anthony de Marchand he has safe passage to my abode — but only if he comes alone."

The messenger turned his back and had just taken his first step toward the forest when the Valkyries returned.

I asked, "What happened?"

Rota answered, "My horse stumbled."

We waited for more. She said nothing but knelt in the snow and inspected the legs of her horse. The other Valkyries were subdued. They stood and stroked the necks of their mounts, heads bowed.

I stepped up to Rota. "We don't understand. What does that mean?"

She answered, "My horse stumbled." As though that should explain all.

We waited. She looked up at us, then shook her head at our denseness and tried again. "My horse stumbled, while we were flying..."

We still did not understand. She went on, "Horses never stumble in flight — there is nothing to stumble upon."

Again we waited, needing more.

"Something is wrong — not with the horse. Something is wrong — not with the dragons. Something is wrong — with this planet."

A few of the other Valkyries came to her and wrapped her in their arms. A half-dozen naked women stood ankle deep in the new snow and softly moaned.

Now what? They were our only hope.

Rota stepped out from the huddle, her horse beside her. "We must fix whatever is broken. What are the religions here?" She looked toward Signe.

Signe opened her mouth but no words came at first. Finally she said, "I don't know."

I explained, "They have none. Nowhere on this planet is there an organized religion."

Rota's voice was firm. "Someone is messing with things."

She ran the few steps to catch the messenger. "Hey you," she said, "what gods do you pray to?"

The messenger looked bewildered, not knowing what she meant.

Rota let him go. But she was still undeterred. "Someone on this planet is messing with things."

THE TRUCE

Anthony de Marchand — self-styled Lord of the North — walked confidently up to the abode of Winter Chief Juha. He did not come alone. But he and his five followers did come unarmed.

The snow continued, driven by a winter wind, falling more laterally than vertically.

We met the delegation and entered the abode of the Winter Chief: me, Juha the Winter Chief of the fifth valley of the Björkan, the Elders Signe and Hildor, Torn the warrior, and Rota the Valkyrie.

The men with Anthony de Marchand stared hard at Rota. Not at her sword — silver sharp and always in her hand — and not at her long mess of hair. No, they stared at her nakedness — or maybe at the snow melting off her nakedness.

Anthony de Marchand broke the spell. "I offer a truce."

Torn answered, "Pack up your men and leave and we will have peace."

Anthony de Marchand stood with his arms down and his palms forward. "I cannot. It is a seven-day march across the stony plain. Out in the open the dragons would feast upon us. I would lose half my army."

Hildor replied, "If you stay, in a hundred days you will have lost it all."

Anthony de Marchand asked, "Can't you tell a story or something — use your magic to put them back in the trees?"

Signe spoke, her voice quiet and calm. "The dragons are their own story; the björka trees are their own story. The balance that has held this world together is its own story. We can tell variations, we can play with metaphors. But when the balance is broken — when the björka is chopped down and the dragon has taken wing — we cannot tell it back. Even we who have kept the stories, we who remember that which was told to us by our grandmothers and great-grandmothers and great-great-grandmothers, have forgotten the language in which those first stories were told."

The tip of Rota's sword was pointed to the ground. She had been resting upon it like a cane. Now she raised it to her shoulder. "There is another problem here — someone has been messing with things."

She pointed her sword at a shorter, dark-skinned man. "Who is this?"

Anthony de Marchand introduced him. "This is Torsten Steelhand."

Torsten bowed to Rota.

Signe handed Torsten a bone and bead choker and he put it on. I was impressed that he did not show pain.

Hildor explained to Rota, "He is of the Hakkapeliitta — they are mercenaries who fight for money."

Torsten retorted, "I expect to be paid for my service, but I fight for honour."

Torn spit. "Whose honour? Yours or the man who pays you?"

Torsten spoke in a clear, calm voice, "I uphold the honour of the Hakkapeliitta people. We never quit; to surrender would shame us all."

Signe spoke to Rota, but also to the room. "The Hakkapeliitta story is powerful and proud. From it the people draw their strength. They say, 'We will never quit.' That is their salvation and their destruction. It saves them because they need to be strong to persevere in their climate. It destroys them because the parasites from the south come and buy their services, knowing they will never quit. They fight in all the wars and die in all the wars; their story will remain strong until the last of them falls."

Torsten nodded to Signe. "Elder," he said, "you are wise and can see much, but we are more than a story. We have our own magic. It is not raw determination that brings us through the battle. We are protected; we are blessed."

Rota screamed, "Who protects you? Who says you are blessed?"

Torsten Steelhand stepped away from the scream and away from the tip of Rota's sword.

Rota continued, "Who, damn you, who?"

Torsten set his jaw firm, straightened his back, and stepped forward. He put his chest to the tip of Rota's blade, held his arms down and his palms forward. He said, "My dear lady, I am protected by magic summoned by the shaman Kyyran Jussi."

Rota calmed herself and asked, "Where can I find this Kyyran Jussi?"

Torsten answered, "In the village of Turku."

Hildor offered, "Cross the stony plain and turn west. Follow the treeline for eight days until you come to a river. Follow the river another two days until it reaches the sea. The village of Turku is on the high ground. You can't miss it."

Rota stepped out of the Winter Chief's abode. She screamed, "Kyyran Jussi! Kyyran Jussi!" The other Valkyries joined in.

They flew away
in a frenzy
screaming,
"Kyyran Jussi!
Kyyran Jussi!
Kyyran Jussi!"
as they went.

.   .   .

The Valkyries returned in less than an hour. Anthony de Marchand and his men were still preparing to leave while the dragons continued their afternoon nap.

Kyyran Jussi — the shaman — was tossed unceremoniously from the back of a Valkyrie's horse into the snow in front of the abode of the Winter Chief. He immediately sprang to his feet, evidently much younger than he appeared.

He demanded, "What is this? Who dares to kidnap me? Is it you?" He faced Anthony de Marchand. "I'll have you know I am not afraid of your guns or the magic of aliens."

Anthony de Marchand replied, "It's not me, old friend. I'm just trying to avoid becoming supper for a dragon."

Kyyran Jussi looked around quickly. "What dragons?" he asked.

Signe answered, "Hello, Kyyran. It's true: Anthony

de Marchand and his men chopped down the björka trees and freed the dragons."

"Shit," was all Kyyran said.

Rota pointed her sword at Kyyran's face but she spoke to Signe. "Do you have another bone and bead choker so I can talk to this man?"

Signe did.

Kyyran Jussi said, "I know what this is," as he put it on. "I'm not afraid of a little pain."

Rota raised the tip of her sword to Kyyran's face. "You will fear this." Her voice sounded soft though stern — maybe because she wasn't screaming. "You are as much at fault for the release of the dragons as the invaders." She pointed at Anthony de Marchand.

"Me?" Kyyran Jussi looked surprised.

Rota's voice rose, but not to a scream — not yet. "Yes, you. Damn it. You've been messing with things you do not understand."

Kyyran inhaled sharply and took a quarter step backward. Everyone present could see the accusation was true. But what was there to do? Letting Rota kill him wouldn't fix anything.

Kyyran lowered his head and looked at his feet in the snow — likely to take his eyes from the tip of Rota's sword.

Signe spoke. "Kyyran, you are among the Björkan people. I assure you, you are among friends. But you must tell us what it is you have done."

Kyyran looked up. "I didn't think," he said. "I found an old song of power and sang it for these men. I should have listened to my inner voice, which told me not to." He lowered his head again for a moment, then admitted, "It was arrogance. I had a song of power and wanted to show it off. I forgot to be humble."

"You are a human," Signe told him. "Humans make mistakes."

Kyyran Jussi raised his head and said, "How do I make this right? I cannot unsing the song."

It was only then that
   it became clear to me
      what had happened here.
     The balance,
       the song, and
         how things had gone so wrong.

This shaman Kyyran Jussi should have known better. The universe is only a vibration. We are a ripple in the essence. I imagined him with his hand drum and an ancient song of power, manipulating the universe's vibration in his favour.

Anthony de Marchand and his men — these mercenaries, these Hakkapeliitta — marched to the beat of a song out of tune with the universe. When they cut the trees, they swung their axes to the beat. It was discordance that set the dragons free. I wondered what happened to the symmetry. Usually the vibration of the

universe causes all things to vibrate at the same rate —
in tune, like a single singer in a choir. Their voice will
not stay discordant — it will be brought along, drawn
into the song.

So what happened here?

Kyyran Jussi's ancient verse,
 out of tune with
  the one verse of
   the universe.

One verse —
 universe,
  one verse —
   universe.

My mind followed the rhythm. One song — one
song. I asked, "Do we have singers? We need powerful
singers."

Anthony de Marchand looked toward Juha and
asked, "What about those men you placed on the ice
to lull us to sleep?"

"The Spelmen," Juha replied.

Signe was quick. "Yes! Yes!" she said. "Where are
the dragons now? We could send the Spelmen to settle
them down."

"They're at the confluence," Anthony de Marchand
answered. "That's where they sleep."

I said, "We'll need more than just Spelmen and
nyckelharpor. They can hold the dragons — for now.

But to restore the balance and sing the dragons back into the trees will take a powerful song and a powerful voice."

My next thought made me laugh. It was so silly, but it might work and the universe would get a chuckle from it too. I caught Rota giving me the eye and smiled.

THE PEACE

"No," Irja said. "No — no — no." Then she smiled and said, "Oh no. You are not nice, Lilly — giving this task to me."

I replied, "You are the only one. If this task can be done, Irja, it can only be you."

Irja shook her head, still smiling. "I can't believe it," she said. "I'm going to teach Valkyries to sing. The universe is truly a strange place."

Then she became serious as she thought it through. She asked, "Is there bitter root on the ship? I thought there was, but I'm not sure."

"Yes, there is. On the edge of the little pond. I know because I planted it there," I answered.

"That's good," Irja said. "I have a feeling the Valkyries are going to need a lot of bitter root to soothe their voices."

In the days
　　in between
　　　　I had time to visit,
　　　　　to sit and
　　　　　　drink tea and
　　　　　　converse
　　　　　　　with Juha.
We spoke in generalities, avoiding talk of what could have been. He told me stories, often funny — spirit lifters designed to bring a smile. There was hope in his voice. He could imagine his people once again living peacefully and safely in their valley.

We could hear the songs of the Spelmen up on the ice — singing to the dragons, lulling them to sleep. Occasionally we heard a discordant screech, as Irja tried to teach the Valkyries to sing.

The dragons snoozed. Except for the swallow tail. She paced. She nudged her sleeping fellows, grabbed them by the shoulders and shook, roared at them and stamped her feet.

But they did not wake.
　　Dragons are not smart and
　　　dragons are not stupid.
The swallow tail attacked the Spelmen, drove them from the ice. When the music and the song died, her brothers and sisters awoke. And when the dragons awoke they were hungry.

"I need to understand dragons," Torn spoke to Rota. "What do you know of them?"

Rota replied, "To kill a dragon you must drive your blade between its plates. And remember to avoid the flame."

"But how," Torn asked, "do they make their fire?"

Rota answered, "It's just a belch. Their guts are rotten and give off flammable gases. They ignite the gases by sparking their front teeth. If you can get one to belch three or four times, they usually run out of gas. But not always. Never — ever — stab a dragon in the guts. You might think you are attacking the soft underbelly, but you're likely to cause an explosion and your sword will stink for years after. And whatever you do, don't get any of that stink on you — it doesn't wash off and you'll be left without any friends."

Torn was thoughtful. He spoke in an even tone, though his eyes said something different. "So the flames come from their burps. What then makes Dragon Blood so explosive?"

Rota explained in a tone as balanced as Torn's, but her eyes, too, spoke of something else, something more. "What you gather from the occasional björka tree is not blood. It's just called that because it's red. What you call Dragon Blood is the essence of a dragon. When I kill a dragon — when my blade finds its heart — its blood is as wet and sticky as any other."

Rota looked up at the grey sky and the thick, falling snow. An idea formed in her mind. She asked, "How much of this stuff you call Dragon Blood do you have?"

"I am told we have several barrels," Torn replied.

"I only need one." Rota began to laugh. "Oh, and I need rope — lots of rope."

I asked, "What's your plan?"

Rota answered, "I plan to outsmart a dragon."

She flew away, with a barrel of Dragon Blood on a long rope trailing behind.

. . .

Rota's plan worked, sort of. When she approached the swallow tail dragon from the sky, it took the bait. It chased Rota. And when it was close, it snorted fire at her. As planned, the barrel of Dragon Blood exploded and the swallow tail was knocked from the sky.

But when the dragon fell, she landed in the circle of abodes where the children and the women were sheltering. She bounced when she hit the ground, and something inside her broke. But she managed to stand, dragging her left wing, and she hopped about in a rage grabbing at the children.

A wail rose from the women. A child had been caught. I could not tell whose child from the wailing — all the women grieved the same. They each picked up a remaining child and, still wailing, held it to their chests and began to slowly rise into the air, out of reach of the swallow tail.

The dragon held the child in its claw pinned to the ground. I saw the child struggle. I saw the Valkyries circle overhead about to dive. I saw Torn attack straight at the dragon's head, and I saw Juha running, his blade in his hand. He told the story of how he slew the dragon as he ran. As he leapt over the split tail and up the dragon's back — his blade in both hands now — he pointed its tip downward. Torn swung at the dragon's nose. When she reared back, Juha drove his blade between the plates where neck met shoulder.

When the dragon fell, Torn grabbed the child and ran. Juha rolled clear as the Valkyries descended. They attacked in a horde — steel blades and Valkyrie screams — and soon the swallow tail dragon was dead.

A group of dragons is not called a rage for nothing. When the swallow tail fell, the other dragons swarmed in anger. Their roar came not only from their throats, but also from their fire.

The women still holding children had sought safety in the air from the crashed swallow tail. And now the remaining dragons prepared to descend upon them. But that's why we brought Valkyries — twenty-three screaming women with swords and horses and a deep desire to kill dragons.

They were not alone in the battle: Åke brought

out the archers, who sped their arrows skyward. The women from my ship sang together, found the sound of the universe, and put it into voice to give strength to the Valkyries.

The women of the fifth valley fled into the forest with the children. I saw Juha and Hildor tell the story of the battle as it unfolded. They told a toppled Valkyrie back onto her horse; they told a dragon to miss as it clawed at a rider.

. . .

Valkyries will ride in darkness but dragons will not. Sunset brought the battle to its end. Two dragons and three Valkyries were dead.

During the night we grieved for our fallen. The injured child was ministered to — he would have scars on his chest and back, but he would live. And like Signe said, he would have a story to tell.

One of the Valkyries
     killed in battle
          had been eaten.

The bodies of the other two were collected — one from the ice, the other from the river. I offered to take them back to the ship, but Rota said they could be placed under a björka tree in the way of the people here. Sigrun and Herja were placed under the same tree to keep each other company.

And of Sigrun's horse that survived the fall, Rota said they would take it back with them.

We planned throughout the night. The Valkyries would continue the fight if we asked, but they were bloodied. Their spirits were not broken, but they were badly bruised. We needed another way to fight the dragons that wouldn't mean losing more of our friends.

When dawn arrived — when the dragons first began to stir — we were ready. The Spelmen were on the ice again putting music and song into the first light. The shaman Kyyran Jussi drummed a healing song as he walked toward the dragons, one careful step at a time. Juha led the warriors, though not into battle; they did not draw their blades. They walked behind the shaman Kyyran Jussi and told a story — a long and complicated story of dragons and björka trees.

The Valkyries flew — this time without screaming — and sang, their voices beautiful in the cold, crisp dawn.

I later asked Irja how she'd done it — how she'd taught the Valkyries to sing.

She said, "I asked them how they kept their horses in the air. They said they didn't know — they just did. So I told them to do the same thing with their voices, and they began to sing."

My ship-sisters and I assisted — but only later, once the dragons began to take root. We know about planting, how to nurture a seedling along, how the life in the seed needs to connect with the life in the earth. We sprinkled those first roots with living water, and soon the life in the dragons connected with the life of the planet.

When it was done, when the Valkyries finished their song, when Kyyran Jussi put down his drum and the Spelmen put down their nyckelharpor — when the story of the dragons and the björka had been told — eight björka trees stood at the confluence where eight dragons had stood before.

THE END

The dragons were planted, but we were not yet done.

Kyyran Jussi had earned his redemption with his song and his drum. He had undone the rift he had created — the rip in the fabric of the universe that allowed dark power to flow into this world. We allowed him to go home, but he had to walk and walk alone so that he would learn to listen.

Anthony de Marchand needed to answer for all that he had done. One of the Valkyries suggested that he be shot with one of his own guns. But the people of the valleys had had enough of death, enough of dying, enough of bodies being laid to rest against björka trees.

"It's greed," said Signe.

"He wants more than he needs," added Hildor.

"Something needs to be done about the guns," said Juha.

"We can take them," I offered.

"But you can't take the idea," said Torn. "To get rid of the guns we will have to get rid of everyone who knows how to build one. We'll have to kill Anthony de Marchand and all of his men and all of the metal workers in Mora. And we would have to kill all of us as well because now we know about guns. Ideas are harder to kill than dragons."

We all nodded — the women of the medicine ship, the Valkyries, who knew the most about battle, all of the Björkmen and all of the Björkwomen. Even Anthony de Marchand and several of his men nodded.

I felt responsible. It was I who had brought the aliens to this planet. I should have known better. I know about invasive species, how a single spore can alter an entire ecosystem. I thought of a planet we'd once found. It had been lush and rich. The next time we came it was completely dead. We must have introduced a disease that the planet could not defend against. It had wiped out every living thing there, and when the disease had nothing left to infect, it, too, died in the end.

I was about to say that the people here would have to develop an immunity toward guns, but I didn't have to. Signe spoke instead. "Ideas are part of the essence of the universe — it was an idea that became the first sword and an idea that became the first arrow. You men…" She looked around, not just at Anthony de Marchand and his men, but at the Björkan men too. "We've kept a secret from you because you didn't need to know. And as long as you were warriors, you couldn't use it anyway."

She closed her eyes, wrapped her arms around herself, and gently rose into the air. All the women present — even the Valkyries, who had just learned to sing — ululated in unison. Our loud trill accompanied her ascension. When Signe reached the tops of the björka trees, she opened her eyes, spread her arms, and gently descended.

"We can teach you this," she said. "But to do it, you will have to give up being warriors. It cannot be done if there is any anger in the body. You must learn to love to learn to fly. Your choice: you can learn to fly or you can learn to die."

Again all the women ululated out of sheer exuberance.

Juha spoke, "The men will help. We will tell a story to go with the teaching. No one will be able to fly if they have held a gun in the last year."

He turned to Anthony de Marchand and his men. "You, too, can have this — this gift from the Björkan women — but you have to put away your guns and do penance for one whole year."

And so it was,
    as they said
      in the end,
        their choice to
        be a killer
          or an angel.

I asked Juha to come back with me, but he said he had to fulfill his tenure as Winter Chief. It wasn't his choice; it was a duty put upon him by the people. I was Ship Mother. I had to go back.

We returned to our vessel — seven medicine women, twenty Valkyries, and Torn, who had, as a wedding gift from Rota, the horse that had carried Sigrun into battle.

Juha was going to be busy rebuilding the fifth valley of the Björkan. It would take at least until the end of his term as Winter Chief. But at the next equinox, the moment he lays down his staff, I intend to be there.

Until then, Juha,

until then.

Love, Lilly.

EPILOGUE

I did not go down to Prince Albert on Friday to pick up Joe's ashes. I phoned and put it off, partly because it had rained heavily the day before and the road south would be all mud, and partly because I first wanted to read Joe's sagas.

When I finally made the trip, the coroner handed me Joe's ashes in a cardboard box. Mind you, the box was dignified, dark grey and sturdy, but it was still made out of cardboard. I don't think Joe would have cared too much.

It was a two-hour drive home to Molanosa from Prince Albert, so I had lots of time to think about what Joe would have wanted done with the ashes. The cardboard box sat on the passenger seat next to me. I tried talking to it as though it was still Joe.

"What do you want me to do with you?"

The box didn't answer.

"Sprinkle you on the water, eh? Is that what you want? I'm not taking you home and keeping you. You know that."

No answer.

"I'm going to miss you, you old bugger."

I thought about that. It was going to be different. Even though Joe wasn't someone I went to visit often, wasn't someone I hung out with regularly, it had been nice having Joe around, knowing I had a neighbour just down the river a ways. Someone I could go visit if I wanted to, someone I could hang out with for an afternoon, someone close by, a friend.

My world had shrunk. It was a tiny bit smaller now that a piece of it was missing.

By the time I got back to Molanosa, drove the boat downriver, and tied it up to Joe's little dock, I knew what needed to be done with the ashes. In his saga, Joe's Björkans were placed under a björka tree to continue their final journey. I would put Joe's ashes under the old spruce tree.

I know, I know, björka is the Swedish word for birch. If I was following the script, I should have put Joe's ashes under a birch tree. But he had died under a spruce. That was his choice. He wanted to emulate the wolf, and the wolf had chosen a spruce. So spruce it was, the same one just down the shore from his cabin.

At first, I thought to dump the ashes on the ground, but I decided to leave them inside the box instead. It was cardboard, it would compost. A little rain would soften it up, then insects and mycelia would tear it apart, draw it back into the soil. The spruce tree's roots would pick up the atoms from the soil and carry them up toward the sky, and Joe's journey across the universe would continue after its brief, one-hundred-and-one-year stop on this planet.

Then another question hit me: What was to be done about his cabin?

"Damn you, Joe. You make me do things I don't want to do."

I liked Joe's cabin. It was made from hand-hewn logs, with axe marks all along the flat sides. I especially liked the dovetail corners. There aren't many people left who know how to make a decent-fitting dovetail notch. But it couldn't stay. It would be too tempting for someone to move in; someone who would not keep and respect the memory Joe had created here. No, the cabin had to go. It had to pass from this world like its creator, or maybe along with its creator.

The quickest thing would be just to light it up. Cremate it. The forest was wet, so there would be little risk of starting a forest fire. But the smoke would attract attention. There would be a helicopter with a fire crew on the scene within minutes. Helicopters are noisy and they burn gasoline. I don't think Joe would have liked that.

Instead, I climbed onto the roof of Joe's cabin and chopped through the ridge pole with his axe. With a hole in the roof, the rain would get in. Nature would take care of the rest. A wooden building can stand for a long time if it has a good roof and a dry foundation. It won't last long with a hole in the roof. The rain and the bugs and the mould and the mycelia take it down and return it back to the earth in no time at all.

I was going to prop the door open and leave, but then I decided to have one more look around. Nothing had changed. No one had been there. Not that anyone *should* have been there. Joe didn't get many visitors; I didn't expect anyone to be dropping by. I hadn't posted notices of his death, so even the people who knew Joe weren't aware that he wasn't with us anymore. His cabin wasn't visible from the river, so people passing by in boats during the summer wouldn't be stopping to check it out. No, Joe's cabin would likely crumble and go back to the earth without anyone noticing.

Inside, there was a shelf of books in the bedroom. I checked the titles. Isaac Asimov's *Azazel*; Leo Tolstoy's *A Confession* and *The Kingdom of God Is Within You*; Henry George's *Progress and Poverty*; Karl Marx's *Kapitalet*, translated into the Swedish by Rickard Sandler in 1930; and several Louis L'Amour westerns, including *Show Down at Yellow Butte* and *Where the Long Grass Blows*. I wondered at a man who read books like these: Asimov's futurism, Tolstoy's pacifism, Marx's revolutionism, and L'Amour's American frontierism.

It was none of my business, but I looked through Joe's closet. It didn't hold much: his good winter coat, a few shirts and sweaters, a pair of blue overalls. His .30-30 Winchester stood leaning against the corner. I levered the action to make sure it wasn't loaded. In the opposite corner to the rifle, tucked away out of sight, sat an ammunition box, one of those military surplus metal boxes with a flip-up lid. On the lid was stencilled "Juha Tossavainen." *Juha must be the Swedish for Joe*, I thought. I set the box on the little dresser by the bed and opened it, expecting to find ammunition for the rifle. Instead, I found a .45-calibre Browning pistol and seven magazines of ammunition. *What the hell was Joe doing with something like this?*

I carefully lifted the pistol out of the box and saw that there was something wrapped in red cloth hiding underneath. I pulled back a corner of the cloth and let out an audible gasp. Inside, I found a bone and bead choker.

I buried the rifle, pistol, and ammunition where they wouldn't be found. The moisture and the soil's acidity would take care of them: within a few months, they'd be covered in rust, and after a few years they'd be completely unrecoverable.

I hadn't intended to keep anything of Joe's that he had not expressly given to me. I could easily have taken the little canoe, the Sony radio made in Ireland, the rifle and the pistol. No one would ever question how I got them. But to me it was simple: they weren't mine; I had no right to them.

But the bone and bead choker — that was something different. Though I had no right to it, I was going to keep it anyway. I can't say how, but a part of me knew that someday I would need it. And I figured Joe would want me to be prepared.

ACKNOWLEDGEMENTS

I need to thank all of the wonderful people who were part of the evolution of this work. It started as a story I told myself each night before I went to sleep. I put the story into the dream world and this is what I found in the morning when I woke up and began writing it. Others, especially Sean Virgo, helped me to reshape the story, to bring it into focus. My wife, Joan, heard all of the first drafts and kept the dream alive. Douglas Richmond smoothed the rough edges. Kris Faller entered the dream with me. Stephanie Sinclair carried the story a distance, and Samantha Haywood carried it to its final destination. Thank you to Bruce Walsh, who believes in dreams, and to my beautiful cousin Pia Enocson for the Swedish interpretation.

HAROLD R. JOHNSON is the author of five works of fiction and five works of nonfiction, including *Firewater: How Alcohol Is Killing My People (and Yours)*, which was a finalist for the Governor General's Literary Award for Nonfiction. Born and raised in northern Saskatchewan to a Swedish father and a Cree mother, Johnson served in the Canadian navy and has been a miner, logger, mechanic, trapper, fisherman, tree planter, and heavy equipment operator. A graduate of Harvard Law School, he managed a private practice for several years before becoming a Crown prosecutor. Johnson is a member of the Montreal Lake Cree Nation. He is now retired from the practice of law and writes full-time.